Martine Murray was born in Melbourne, Australia,
where she still lives and has just won the Queensland
Literary Premiers Award. She started writing because she
had a very nice dog she wanted to write about.

Cedar B. Hartley, Upside Down was her first novel about
Cedar and was shortlisted for several awards in Australia.

CEDAR B. HARTLEY
FLYING HIGH

MARTINE MURRAY

MACMILLAN CHILDREN'S BOOKS

First published in Australia 2005 as *The Slightly Bruised Glory of Cedar B. Hartley*

First published in the UK 2007 by Macmillan Children's Books
a division of Macmillan Publishers Limited
20 New Wharf Road, London N1 9RR
Basingstoke and Oxford
www.panmacmillan.com

Associated companies throughout the world

ISBN: 978-0-230-01430-5

1 3 5 7 9 8 6 4 2

A CIP catalogue record for this book is available from
the British Library.

Typeset by Tou-Can Design
Printed and bound in Great Britain by Mackays of Chatham plc, Kent

For Mum and Dad,
with love

At the station

I'm at Spencer Street train station. It's the big one, where trains come in from all over the country. What's more, you wouldn't believe it if you could see me. You wouldn't believe it was me. You'd say, 'Now is that really Cedar B. Hartley? My, hasn't she grown up.' That's the way you'd say it if you were over fifty. But otherwise you might just think to yourself, 'Hmmm, that girl, she's not a kid anymore.'

I'll tell you one thing: I'm wearing an apple-green sundress, and it's hot and it's nearly Christmas. Well, that's three things, and I won't say one thing more about why I'm here in my green dress at the train station. First I have to tell you about the terrible, terrible thing that happened, and everything else that led me here.

Chapter 1

There's me and there's Kite, and then there's all the others. That's not in order of importance because the others are just as important as Kite and almost as important as me, though not quite, because I'm me after all, and to myself I'm extremely important; not because I'm in love with myself or anything, just because I made a plan to live an unusual life, and in order to live an unusual life you need to do a lot of discovering and uncovering and maybe recovering too. Who knows? So, I'm always asking myself: just what kind of shape is my life in? Is it getting flabby? Or is it getting close to the particular shape that I plan it to take?

See, I have always favoured the shape of a tree, but not a pine tree; a pine-tree-shaped life is not for me. I am Cedar B. Hartley and let it be known that I would prefer to live my life in the shape of a golden elm tree, more specifically the one on Punt Road that spreads out so much you can't even see the trunk. There are certain people who might have a pine-tree-shaped life, but I don't like to name names (like

Marnie and Harold Barton) because a pine-tree-shaped life doesn't spread out but just goes up in a narrow point. If you thought about my best friend, Caramella, you might see her life in the shape of a fruit tree; not big, but full of beautiful, quiet fruits. And Oscar is a willow tree because he stands out in a particular way, and you can't help loving the particular way he stands out, even if it doesn't always make sense, even if it leans over a little too much.

As for Kite, I'd say he's in the shape of a river red gum, tall and towering and true. And if that leads you to suppose that I might have a small crush on Kite, you're absolutely wrong. I haven't got a small crush on Kite, I've got quite a big one; a crush the size of a huge wave that only Layne Beachley could surf. Have you heard of Layne Beachley? She's a famous lady surfer. We girls have to stick together and celebrate heroes like Layne Beachley and Mother Teresa, who also did great things like helping the needy. Also, don't forget Marge Manoli, the Op Shop Lady in Smith Street who from here on in shall represent the countless thousands of kind-hearted ladies who won't ever be famous, since kindness isn't as exciting as surfing or winning the one-day match with a hat trick, and what's more you can't really watch it on telly.

But I'm sorry, God, it's not kindness that I'm going to be famous for. What I plan to become is *infamous*. An infamous acrobat. Like Kite.

Infamous is more famous than famous, don't forget that. You may want to use it one day yourself. Though don't say it in front of your big brother or he may laugh in a slightly scoffing way, like my brother Barnaby does. Barnaby is mostly just jealous because he's really crappy at cartwheels and has to count on being a famous rock star instead of an acrobat. He's always in his bedroom writing love songs on his guitar because he's either in love again or he's out of love again, and both states of being seem to require him to sing about it. Maybe all songs are about love, and even if they're called dust-bowl ballads and they seem to be about people without land they're still really about love. Anyway, Barnaby is pretty good at getting love because he's clever and he's good at footy and he's also a little bit handsome, but don't tell him I said that. Lucky for Barnaby, he inherited dark hair from our father, who died when we were kids. But as for me, I'm not so lucky. I'm a redhead like our Aunt Squeezy. Her real name is Tirese but I call her Squeezy. I'll tell you more about Aunt Squeezy later because I know what you really want to hear about now is Kite.

So here goes.

First of all, Kite has a voice like a river running by. Second of all, he can move like an animal. Thirdly, he's very cool, and when I say cool what I really mean is warm. Isn't that funny? He's cool in a warm way. I mean he's cool because he isn't afraid to be warm. He doesn't wear new clothes; he just wears camel corduroys or King Gees. And he knows what he's interested in and it doesn't matter to him what anyone else is interested in. Whereas Harold Barton is always getting the latest thing, like the fattest best skateboard, even though he isn't the best skateboarder. Ricci says Harold Barton has a little dog complex. If you're a little dog, best thing is to bark all the time, especially if you see a big dog. That way you'll have a large effect, which will compensate for your small presence. You don't often hear Harold Barton barking, which is a shame because at least that would be amusing, but what you do hear from Harold is a lot of bragging and bad-mouthing. Unfortunately, that can have a large effect because it makes you mad when he calls your best friend Zit-face, or he calls Oscar The Spaz, or me No-hoper Hartley. Sometimes I feel like giving him a big thump, but lucky for Harold I'm in training to become a Buddhist and that means I can't thump him. Instead I must feel compassion for him.

Compassion is not like passion, because it's not so thumping hot, so you have to take your temperature down to warm, and then you have to summon feelings of kindness and understanding. I can tell you, it's very challenging to feel kindness and understanding for someone you want to thump. It's harder than maths, butterfly swimming, map reading and horse riding.

picture of a cactus
trying to be a
buddhist

Here's something I'm bad at: feeling compassion for Harold Barton.

Not to worry, I still have my whole life to master this compassion game. There's no shortage of little-dog-bad-mouthers and prissy-poodle-know-alls (Marnie) so I'll have to practise transforming my thumping urge over and over again. And, just for the record, I'm not calling Marnie anything, since I don't want to become a bad-mouther myself, but really, is there anything more annoying than a know-all?

As for me, I'm a know-nothing.

Except for one or two things I do know. If you want to be good at guitar, you have to fall in love a lot and sing songs in your bedroom. Another thing I know is that it's hard to work out who you are, and it doesn't matter if you make a mistake. Also I know how to do a cartwheel.

You know what I just thought? (This isn't something I know, this is just a little stumbling philosophy according to Cedar B. Hartley, which happens every now and then, but don't worry, I'm not planning on becoming a philosopher because a philosopher can't be an acrobat, and a philosopher has to become serious and ponderous and wonder about things that other people can't be bothered wondering about, and who would want to hang out with you if you were that serious? Anyway, this is my first guess in the realm of philosophy.)

It's all about love.

Everything somehow depends on love, or is sad without it, or wants more than anything to find it.

Some people do strange things because of love. They become brave, or they go on diets, or they give away their favourite CD.

And love comes in different colours. Some of those colours just strike you with their brightness, while others are soft, or unremarkable, like the muddy, worn colour of your sneakers. But still you need that colour. You need its familiarity. You depend on it without even knowing, until one day something terrible happens, and then you see just how much you do need those familiar colours around you.

Which brings me back to Kite.

Chapter 2

The terrible, terrible thing happened because of me, in an indirect way, which makes sense because most things I do are in a round-about, indirect kind of curly way. That's because I'm a wanderer and I can't bear to stay on the main road.

Here's how it went.

First of all, I was a skinny twelve-year-old redhead with a dog called Stinky and a lot of things to find out. Then I met Kite. That's how I became Cedar B. Hartley, not-yet-famous acrobat in a small circus called The Acrobrats.

It was Kite who showed me how to become an acrobat. But it was me who showed Kite that we could make a circus. Life's great like that. It's like a big game where you have to join forces because, let's face it, you can't be good at everything. And there's a load of things I, for one, am very bad at. Here's a list:

Feeling compassion for Harold Barton.

Anything that requires patience, like sewing.

Keeping my big mouth shut.

Maths, science, map reading, sticking to timetables, remembering homework and swimming butterfly, though my backstroke isn't bad.

Horse riding, because I never had a horse, though if someone has a spare one they don't want anymore I'll look after it with great tenderness. Also, if you have a dog that needs looking after I can do that too, but don't tell Mum I said so.

picture of a tenderly looked after horse in horse pyjamas

Chess, cards, Monopoly and most other sitting-down games, apart from Snap, which I love because it gets me excited.

Not losing things. For instance, every summer I lose my sunnies about fifty times.

Keeping my bedroom tidy. You should see Caramella's bedroom. It's lovely. But how does anyone manage to put their clothes away once they take them off? I always think I'll do it later, and then I forget.

✿   ✿   ✿

I won't go on because if you go on and on about what you're bad at you can start to believe it matters, and if anything is going to matter it's not what you're bad at but what you're good at.

Kite is good at tree climbing and all sorts of acrobatics. Also, he's good at being calm.

Oscar is good at being berserk and original.

Caramella is good at art and at being a best friend.

Barnaby is good at making up songs and being charming and therefore at getting away with stuff other people wouldn't get away with.

Ricci is good at knowing old-fashioned knowings and at cooking stews.

Mum is good at caring for others and putting up with me.

I'm good at thinking up ideas.

And jumping.

So it was my idea that Kite should teach me acrobatics, and it was my idea to do a circus show with all the others. Then, because the circus went so well, I had the big idea that we could perform it at the community centre, and because a lot of people saw it there, including a certain somebody, the terrible, terrible thing happened.

It happened about six months and two days ago.

Caramella and I were on our way to training. We trained at Kite's house, out the back in his garage, where there are mats and a trapeze. We had my dog Stinky with us, since he always comes whenever I walk anywhere.

The house on the corner of our street belongs to the Abutula family, who come from Afghanistan. That's in the

Middle East, which is a very angry place right now and a lot
of people have to leave it and come and live here instead,
because there are all these arguments going on about who
owns the land. And since it's the adults who are arguing,
there's no mum or dad who can say, 'That's enough, go to
your room, share your belongings, or say sorry and give it
back to the rightful owner.'

The Abutula family came out here a long time ago.
Hailey and Jean Pierre were born here and they're younger
than us so they're not in the circus, but maybe they will be
when they get a bit bigger. Their dad drives a taxi, but Mum
says he's really a doctor and it's a shame he can't practise as a
doctor here because we need more doctors, especially in the
country, in places like the dreaded Albury. Jean Pierre is just
a regular little boy who likes showing off and yelling out,
and Hailey has a rabbit called Madge, so they're pretty nice
kids. But, lately, Caramella and I had been noticing some
strange goings on in the Abutula house. Lots of cars pulling
up and lots of people we didn't know going inside and
coming out again. And we hadn't seen Hailey or Jean Pierre
out on the street. So we were doing just a wee bit of sticky-
beaking on our way past. I was peeking through the fence.
Caramella was keeping watch.

'Can you see anything?' she said.

'Nope, just some toys in the garden, a swing hanging
from the lemon tree and JP's bike.'

'Hmm, weird,' said Caramella, who was second chief

sleuth. Weird because it wasn't weird at all and we were wanting and expecting to find something really weird, like circular burn tracks from a space ship or a toothless person hiding in the lemon tree.

'Wait a minute,' I said. 'Can you hear something?'

We both pressed our ears to a gap in the fence.

'It's music,' said Caramella. 'Strange music.'

'Very strange,' said I, and we both nodded. We were relieved to have discovered more evidence, and as we walked on we pondered this extra clue.

'I think there might have been people dancing inside the house,' said Caramella.

I shook my head. 'No one dances in the afternoon. People only dance in the morning if they are especially happy, or in the night if they're in love, or if they're wanting to be in love.'

'Who said?'

'I did.'

'When did you become an expert on when people dance? Was that when you fell in love?' Caramella giggled, because she's a great tease and she particularly liked to tease me about this very particular issue, ever since the infamous kiss. 'I didn't see *you* dancing.'

'That's because I'm not in love, dummy.'

However, we both knew I was *something*. But you absolutely can't admit it, whatever *it* is. If you admit something it becomes real, and once something is real it can be ruined. Whereas it's much safer if it only exists in your head; it's protected by your skull; it's not out in the open, like a sitting duck, as they say.

The kiss, however, happened right out in the open, and although I didn't see it, since I was too busy being kissed and I had my eyes closed, I knew it was a real thing. A real live kiss. I felt it and it happened to me all at once, and I figure it happened to Kite as well, since it seemed to just happen – bang! – like the immaculate conception (which actually probably didn't happen with a bang, it probably happened very, very quietly, like a lullaby, but anyway you get the idea). Neither of us *made* it happen. It was as if something else was directing the show. In fact if we'd thought about it I don't think we would have done it then and there, just after we finished our circus performance, in front of a whole crowd of people, including der-brains like Harold Barton who just had to go and yell out, 'Lovers!' That made Kite blush and then I blushed and then we were so embarrassed that we haven't ever spoken about it, let alone tried it out again. That kiss was one hell of a sitting duck all right, but still I wouldn't take it back. Nope. No way. Not for anything. Not even for a holiday in Hawaii.

Of course Caramella knows everything, every little detail, every little thought that went through my head while my hand was being held and my mouth was being kissed, but still I can't say straight up, 'I'm in love,' because I'm not sure I know what that is. A crush is different. I know about crushes because they happen all the time; they're so easy to get, you can get one without even really knowing the person you've got one on.

When I was a kid I had a crush on Puff the Magic Dragon, and I reckon Barnaby has a crush on Nick Cave from the Bad Seeds, but I know for sure he wouldn't want to kiss him. Mum has a crush on Hugh Grant, and she'd admit it out loud to anyone. I call these 'public crushes'. They're kind of sturdy but perishable, whereas a private crush is much more interesting and vivid and tender. For instance, there may be a boy on your tram who you only see every now and then, but every time you do your heart starts to make you feel funny. You might have to tell your best friend about this kind of a crush. It's as if you've found a very fragile butterfly and you have let it live in your heart.

I have the most unusual crush of all, of course, because I'm leading an unusual life and so mostly I do things a little bit differently. My crush is on someone who has never ever breathed or wept or bled or farted. His name is Holden Caulfield and he doesn't exist, except as a character in a book that was written years ago, way before I was even born. It's Barnaby's favourite book, so I had to read it too, even though Barnaby thinks I don't really appreciate it 'cause I'm not old enough. I think I do appreciate it, because if ever I could meet Holden Caulfield I'd fall in love in one blow, as long as he didn't sneer or smell bad. (I'd probably forgive him if he smelt bad, but not if he sneered.)

So, it's about the most natural thing in the world to get a
crush. A crush happens upon you the way a pimple does, just
like that – pop! – without you even thinking about it. Only
they're much more fun to focus on. Sometimes I suspect
pimples could even be a result of all that heat a crush can
make, cooking up things inside your head and making little
red lumps out of it, on your skin.

But love…I don't think it gives you pimples. It gives you
other kinds of troubles, even worse than pimples, like
heartbreak, for one. You can read about it in novels. Here's
how I think it works:

For one thing, love doesn't just happen. It takes a while.
And it's real. It's not just a thing you imagine, it's a thing you
do. Things you do for real can get muddy and deep and
scary, and also thrilling. Like playing footy. Or surfing. But
what would I know? I'm too young to really be in love. I'm
only just thirteen. I haven't even been surfing yet, but don't
worry, I intend to.

So, my crush is Kite.

Kite Freeman.

Chapter 3

The kiss wasn't the terrible, terrible thing that happened, but it's relevant because it makes the terrible, terrible thing even more terrible. It happened at the rehearsal.

Caramella and I were late, on account of our sleuthing activities. Kite and Oscar were already there. Oscar was lying flat on his back on Kite's garage floor, and he was singing.

I am the walrus koo koo kchoo, koo koo koo kchoo.

But he's not a walrus; he's just a very tall guy with an acquired brain injury. Before he acquired the injury to his brain, you would have been likely to see him lying on his back singing *koo koo kchoo* because he's naturally berserk in an artistic way. His brain injury just makes him slope when he is standing and walking, and when he talks the words come out slower. But apart from that he's still got the same Oscar soul – it's just harder for him to crank it out. It's as if all the hard drive is still there but the keyboard doesn't work as well, so if you press Control you might not get control. Oscar gave his brain an almighty whack by falling off the

Hills Hoist in his backyard while practising acrobatics, so, if nothing else, take this piece of handy advice from a reckless daredevil like me:

Don't hang upside-down on the Hills Hoist. Also, don't try anything tricky or dangerous like a back flip without someone helping you. There are things you can do with a Hills Hoist (like hang your old teddy bear on it and then spin it around and take a photo of the bear in motion) that are still fun and tickle your brain instead of threatening it.

Anyway, Kite wasn't warming up; he was just sitting with his back against the wall. Kite wears his body in a comfortable, lazy way, so his smile takes ages and ages to happen. He smiled at me then and the smile seemed to frisbee right over towards me in slow motion, and I didn't have to move; it came right towards me and then it got me.

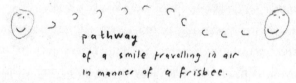

pathway
of a smile travelling in air
in manner of a frisbee.

I loved being got by it.

'Oscar's serenading us,' he said.

Oscar lifted his head slowly as if it was as heavy and awkward as a bowling ball.

'Oh, you two have arrived. Did you notice the grass?'

'No.'

'No, neither did I. There isn't any.' His head clunked back to the ground.

I smiled. Caramella and I took off our shoes.

'There could, however, have been grass and there could have been a duck on the grass and it could have had a straw in its mouth and it could have been trumpeting a song that we all recognised. It could have been singing "I am the Walrus". But unfortunately this wasn't the way it was. There was no grass.'

Caramella said, 'And no duck.'

So far everything was just as it always was; nothing to suggest that something terrible was about to happen. I was swinging my arms around like an excited maypole, Oscar was giving forth on the possibility of ducks, Caramella was still taking her shoes off and Kite was standing up just as if he was about to warm up.

'Where's Ruben?' said Caramella.

'He can't come today,' said Kite.

My arms stopped flapping and fell to my sides. This was the first tremor.

Ruben is Kite's dad and he is also our trainer and our director. He's absolutely perfect for the job. So it was impossible to imagine how we would manage a training session without him. I looked at Kite. He looked at me. And then I knew something had happened. I knew it by the look that went between us, a look that seemed to thud out of his heart and drop to the floor.

'Why can't he come?' I said and I squatted down to steady myself.

'He's in Albury.'

'Albury?' said Caramella. 'You mean Albury-Wodonga? I've been there. It's miles away, halfway to Sydney. There are two towns, one on one side of the river and one on the other. So one is in New South Wales and the other is in Victoria. How's that! We've got cousins there. They've got a café. They make meatballs.'

Obviously, Caramella hadn't yet sensed what I had sensed. She was prattling on as if it was normal for Ruben to be in Albury. Albury-Wodonga.

'Why's Ruben in Albury?' I dropped into chief sleuth mode.

'That's an invigorating place to go,' Oscar bellowed out from his position on the floor.

'Invigorating?' I said, scrunching my nose. 'I bet it's not. I bet it's full of shops selling frocks and car tyres and meatballs and tea towels with native flowers…' I was being a snob about Albury because already I was mad at the town for taking Ruben away from our rehearsal, and I was getting mighty nervous. 'Why is he there?'

Kite was rubbing his neck. Seemed to me he was feeling a bit nervous too.

'He's looking at a house. We're going to live there.'

There it was. He said it. Without even a note of warning. Without even taking the moment in his arms and offering it slowly, tenderly, with some due respect for the momentous blow it could inflict. He just shot the words out his mouth, as if he was spitting out some crumb that had got stuck in a tooth. I had to look at the floor. I saw my feet and they looked like they were going pink, as if the blood was rushing downwards.

'Why are you going to live in Albury?' said Caramella, quietly. She looked up meekly from her sneakers.

Kite kicked at the floor. 'Dad's been offered the job of Artistic Director for the Flying Fruit Fly Circus. You know that one, the professional one. They do shows all round the world. It's a dream job for Dad.'

'But what about you?' I said, looking directly into his eyes.

He took a deep breath in and glanced up at me. 'Cedar, I'm going to join the Flying Fruit Flies. I'll train with them.'

'Oh.' I nodded. Everything felt bad. Now even my face was reddening. I was afraid all my feelings were on show, blazing in my cheeks.

'I have to. What else will I do up there?' Kite shrugged, as if this was all a breezy kind of a thing that had happened. As if it was no big deal. 'You know this wasn't planned. Someone saw our show at the community centre and that was how the offer came through. Dad is very sorry to have to leave our circus here but this is a real opportunity for him, and the contract is only for a year initially so we'll probably be back.'

'You won't be,' said Oscar. 'You'll become a pro. Why would you want to come back here? You'll be in Paris and you'll be flying and…'

He stopped. He had lurched up to sitting, leaning on one arm in a precarious startled way, but then he lay down again and looked up at the ceiling without speaking. For a while no one said anything. I was staring at my red feet. I could hear two people walking by outside and saying things that two people walking together would be likely to say. One said, 'It was that house, I tell you.' And then the other said, 'No it wasn't, it wasn't that house. I should bloody know…' And then I heard Kite saying something. So I had to stop listening to the outside, which was what I preferred to be hearing.

'I'm sorry, guys. In the end it wasn't up to me. I couldn't have said no to Dad.'

'You'll have a good time there, Kite,' said Caramella, so sweetly that I nearly glared at her. Oh why was she being so nice to him, when suddenly I didn't like him at all? How could he go and leave now? Just when we had everything established. Didn't he care? What did he think we were going to do?

I stood up. I was so annoyed I had to stand. I had to do something.

'Well, I guess that's the end of The Acrobrats,' I said, brushing myself down as if I'd got creased from sitting there. I was really brushing away the last crumbs of the circus, *our* circus. Now it was me who was acting like it wasn't a big deal, like oh—well-that's-that, there we go, now who'd like a walk in the park? If Kite didn't care then I wouldn't either.

No way was I going to let this get me. I wanted to walk out of there in one composed piece, gracefully, head held high as high. And then once I was out, I planned on utterly letting my head drop off: smash, kaput, shattering sounds, the whole thing. But you can't do that in a garage, especially when it might betray the size of certain feelings you need to keep small.

I started walking towards the door.

'Hey, Cedar, are you going?' said Kite. He was walking towards me.

'Yeah. I'm going.' I kept backing out. Kite came close and grabbed my hand for an instant, then he let it drop.

'I'm sorry,' he said.

picture of me without
my head on.

Chapter 4

I was meant to say, 'Don't feel bad, Kite, it's not your fault.'
But I didn't say anything. I just dropped my head, spun on
my heel and walked out. For one thing I had the wobbly lip
tremors, which always make you feel like your words have
suddenly got so heavy that they're pressing your mouth into
a quivery unbalanced sobbing shape and, if you let them out,
they'll pour down in a raucous torrent. But also, I didn't
really believe it *wasn't* his fault. I didn't believe that Kite
wasn't excited as hell to be leaving this hotchpotch gang of
small-timers and hitting the big time with real acrobats, real
shining lights, real big tops and real tours of the world. I was
seeing it all, in full glitzy colour, and the glare of it was
hurting my eyes, or maybe it was just that my tears were
making everything shiny and fuzzy, like a Hollywood musical.

Caramella came puffing up behind me. I always walk fast
when I'm upset.

'Hey, wait for me. Are you okay?'

I wiped my eyes and sniffed.

'I'm just mad. I'm mad and I'm sad and I can't think big yet, so I had to leave.'

'It's a first-rate bummer,' said Caramella.

'Yeah.'

'You mad at Kite?'

'Yeah.'

''Cause he didn't tell you first?'

'No. I don't care who he tells. I'm just mad 'cause he doesn't care. He doesn't care about us, not now he's hitting the big time.' I was striding forward with my head down and Caramella was struggling alongside me. I stopped. 'Well, actually, maybe I am mad he didn't tell me first. Should I be? Would you be if you were me?'

'Maybe. Maybe he should have told you because you two started this together and then there's also the kiss and all that...'

'But that doesn't mean anything. That doesn't make any difference.'

I meant this and I didn't mean it. In one way it made all the difference because something had happened between us and that something was hungry. That something had questions and it had ideas and it wanted. But everything went on as if *it* wasn't there, as if *it* made no difference. The only feed the something ever had was once or twice when Kite and I held hands when no one else was around, but that only seemed to keep the something alive without really offering it a place to live.

I guess it wasn't just Kite's fault, though at that moment I felt like blaming him for everything that was making me mad. I didn't really know what to do with a something like that either, but I knew *it* was there and I knew that *it* was making me madder and sadder than anyone else. Because of the kiss, it meant more to me that Kite was leaving.

Sometimes I think that's just the way it is for me. I have a particularly responsive emotional barometer. It's touchy. So when things are good I can almost fly, but when something gets dark and stormy I really know how to let it rain. I just feel things hard, I guess, and that was why I was walking fast and Caramella could barely keep up. I had a lot of emotion to burn. I always had to do something in fast motion when I got that burning feeling inside.

'Hey, don't walk so fast,' she said. 'You know what? I think a kiss does make a difference. I think you should talk to him. That's what I think.'

'I don't feel like talking to him right now.'

'So, you want to come to my place? We've got chocolate macaroons.'

'Aren't you mad, Caramella? Aren't you sad that the circus is over?'

''Course I am,' she shrugged.

Caramella was soft, like a cushion. She could accommodate weight and then just puff back up into shape. She could roll with the punches, as they say. I looked at her in astonishment because I could see she had already bent in

and out and now she was ready to eat chocolate macaroons.
I shook my head.

picture of Caramella
as a cushion

'You know what? I think I have to go home and work
out some stuff in my head because it's really bugging me and
I know I just have to have a big talk with myself about it.
You know what I mean?'

'Sure,' said Caramella. She's a very understanding friend.
That's why I like her. I think somehow we must balance
each other. If we were on a seesaw, her side would be
sensible and calm and sturdy, and my side would be leaping
and dipping and susceptible, but together we can almost
make the seesaw hover in the middle while we dangle our
legs and look at the sky. I say 'almost' because you might
have noticed that right then my side was thrashing around as
if it had come loose in a storm, and even Caramella had not
a hope, not even a chocolate-macaroon-inspired hope of
balancing it up. There was nothing to do but go home and
sit out the bad weather.

Though, of course, this was not what happened.

Chapter 5

Our house was once our Granny's house before she died
from eating too much sugar, so it's half faded and half lively.
I mean it looks like a place that's tried on a few too many
hats; interesting hats, though. There are funny things, like a
used car tyre sitting on top of the letterbox, cut in half,
painted white and planted with pink geraniums. And those
geraniums have to share their tyre house with some claws
of couch grass and the odd fat sow thistle, but they don't
look too mad about it. There's no lawn in the front garden,
just a wild wandering pumpkin vine and also nasturtiums
and some nameless flower bushes and a cluster of giant
green plants with shiny leaves, as big as plates, sitting around
a pond. Barnaby made the pond as part of an installation.
The installation was a kind of aqueduct that carried water
from the downpipes to the pond, though it never really
worked. There are still lonely pieces of wooden pipe
waiting for some water, with pumpkin vine tendrils curled
around them.

picture of house in different hats

There's also an old mustard-coloured couch on the porch, a cape gooseberry plant which Ricci gave us, some jasmine winding round a long stalk of bamboo, a couple of broken bikes leaning against the wall, and two dolls sitting on the windowsill. One is a pear-shaped wooden peasant lady with a scarf, the other is just a plastic green bendy figure who has no features, not even a nose, but it's wound around the sturdy little peasant lady in a passionate embrace. What a pair. You can probably guess who did that to the dolls. The key is above the gas meter and I can reach it by standing on the old shoe-cleaning box. Our door is painted white but the paint is all peeling off in a nice comforting way, and there's a xylophone attached just below the frosted window, with the xylophone banger dangling from a piece of string (yet another Barnaby installation). It's meant to be a doorbell, but most people just yell out.

All this is so familiar to me I hardly ever notice, except when there's something new. Like a lady with red hair sitting on the couch, cross-legged, eyes closed and a faint smile on her face. Smiles don't usually disturb me, but this one did, probably because I was already disturbed and the last thing

I felt like was coming home to a flame-headed vision of peacefulness.

She opened her eyes as I stomped loudly up to the door.

'Oh hello, you must be Cedar.' She unravelled her legs and stood up, stretching her arms and standing on her tippies, just like I do every now and then. Not only that, she was skinny and her hair was untidy and piled up in a knot with bits spilling out. For a minute I wondered if she was me. An older, other version. She wore silver hoops in her ears and she had owl eyes, big and hungry. I watched the way she patted Stinky, because I always like to see whether someone is a dog person. As I've pointed out before, you can trust a dog person, just like you can trust corduroy. She was probably older than Barnaby and younger than Mum.

'That's right,' I said, noticing a big bulging old backpack lying at her feet. 'I'm Cedar. Who are you?'

She smiled at me. I was probably looking like the Black Death, and I didn't feel like smiling back. I looked at the ground. I felt agitated. It was her smile – it seemed to know something I didn't know.

'You probably don't remember me. We have met once before but you were only a baby.'

'So, you're one of Mum's friends?'

'Not yet. I'm your aunt, though I don't feel like an aunt. It's quite odd to say it, really. I guess that's the first time in my entire life I've ever called myself anything as respectable-

sounding as an aunt. Tirese is my name. I'm your dad's sister.
Half-sister, actually.'

The smile broke again. Now I recognised it – it
belonged to my dad. My dead dad. I have a photo of him
with that exact smile, but now it had leapt off my photo and
landed on the face of someone I didn't even know. I wanted
it to stay where it was, in my mind, tucked away in a quiet,
special place that only I could visit. I went there sometimes
and smiled back at my dad. So it was our place, Dad's and
mine, and now someone else was stealing from it. She'd got
his smile and she could wear it, take it with her, any old
place, to flash it at any old person.

I knew my dad had relatives in Western Australia, because
Barnaby went there and met some of them. He never met
Tirese, though, because he would have told me if he had.
He would have remembered her hair.

'I've been in India,' she said, as if by way of explanation,
as I hadn't responded to her announcement except to stand
there with a frown. I didn't exactly feel like meeting an aunt
who'd pinched my dad's smile. I'd had enough shocks for
one day. Couldn't she have come at Christmas or some other
more appropriate time?

She said, 'You probably never even knew I existed. After
all, I didn't even really know your dad.'

'Why didn't you know him?' I was somehow relieved.
She may have his smile but at least she didn't know him.

'Your grandpa remarried when your dad was about

sixteen, and by the time I was born your dad had escaped to Melbourne. So we never knew each other, except through letters and a couple of times when he came home for Christmas. Isn't it funny, though? You and I have the same hair.' She bent down and started putting on an old pair of leather sandals.

'I didn't know him either,' I said.

She folded her arms across her chest and sighed.

'Yes, I know, poor love. Looks like we've got a bit in common then. Shall we have a cup of tea? I've come to stay a while. Do you think your mum will mind? Not too long. Couple of days. I'm just stopping on my way home. Thought I'd visit the other half of the family. I've been away for years.'

Her eyes drifted, like little boats caught in a sudden wind, and I knew she had her own memories tugging her thoughts back. Maybe it didn't matter that she had a part of my dad in her; maybe it would be a good thing. She hauled her pack up and dragged it towards the door as if it was a worn-out, battle-weary body that needed a good rest. I knew then that she'd be staying longer than a couple of days. I'm not sure how I knew, except that it had something to do with that mysterious drifting gaze she had.

Chapter 6

So, all in one day, Kite announced his departure and my skinny Aunt Squeezy announced her arrival, and life started all over again with its onslaught of change.

Mum and I and my new skinny Aunt Squeezy had dinner together that night, and for a while I even forgot about the terrible, terrible thing because, I had to admit, it was interesting to meet my dad's half-sister. I kept watching her curiously and listening to her talking about India, and I was kind of impressed because she had studied loads of weird things in India, like yoga and tabla (a drum that talks) and meditation (sitting down and thinking about nothing, which is harder than you think) and, what's more, she could do a headstand and an elbow stand. Not all aunts can do that. I was glad my dad had a nice half-sister even if he never knew her.

picture of head with thoughts and head with no thoughts

In the end, we moved the chairs in the living room and she showed me some yoga and I showed her some balances and Mum took photos and drank wine. She said wine was just as relaxing as yoga but required less effort. Then she started doing the proud mother thing and telling my aunt all about our circus and our benefit show and I started to feel bad again. I interrupted her.

'Yeah, but Mum it's all over now. Finito. Kite and his dad are moving to Albury. They're joining the Flying Fruit Fly Circus.'

'What's that?' said my new aunt.

'That's a real circus,' I said.

'Oh, Cedy, that's bad luck,' said Mum, 'Can't you go on without them?'

'Nup. No way. Not without a trainer.'

'You'll miss Kite.'

I wasn't sure what my mum knew about Kite. There are some things you just don't tell your mum, and if she suspected something she didn't let on, and neither did I. I didn't answer her. I managed to hold back the emotional torrent, partly by picking at my toenail and partly as a result of all the yoga, which makes you breathe deeply.

'What about finding a new trainer?' said my aunt.

'I don't think we could. We can't pay anyone, and anyway, no one would be as good as Ruben.'

It was actually quite good to find myself talking about it in a practical way, as if suddenly there was simply a problem, as if it was a table with a broken leg and all I had to do was find a way of fixing it. It meant that I could see a way of separating one thing from the other. There were the feelings, the Kite feelings, and they were like air; you couldn't fix them. You can't patch up the air, you can only find ways of making sure you breathe it in and then you breathe it out. (Oh, see how I was already becoming a yogi.)

But then there was also the circus. This was a real thing, not a thing like air but a thing with a broken leg or two. Perhaps this was a thing that could be fixed. Didn't matter that I hadn't a clue how, because right then I wasn't in a mood for working with it, I was in a mood for getting gloomy and staring bug-eyed at the mess. I sighed dramatically and said I had to go to bed, the yoga had made me too relaxed, and they both agreed that bed was a good idea all round. But I think I really kind of killed the mood.

We put my new aunt in Granny's old room, which was still called Granny's room even though she had long since gone from it.

'And what about Barnaby? Where's he?' asked Aunt Squeezy. Mum and I gave each other that look, which meant, 'Who is going to try and explain Barnaby?' I had a go.

'He's got a new girlfriend at the moment. So he's always out with her. You'll meet him tomorrow, probably.'

'Is she nice?'

'She's a Goth,' said Mum.

'Her name's Ada,' I said.

'She's a bit troubled,' said Mum.

'They're in a band together,' said I.

'I see,' said Aunt Squeezy, nodding understandingly, but both Mum and I knew it would take a lot more than that for her to really understand either Barnaby or Ada, let alone what they were together, but we didn't say.

✱ ✱ ✱

Once I was in bed I was glad to be able to finally plummet into my despair in private. It was as if the suffering sat squelched inside me, like a cork, and nothing else could get in and out until that cork had been let loose.

Oh why, I wailed to myself, as I lay in my favourite pondering position on my back, staring at the ceiling, why must I constantly adapt? You work so hard to get things just right and then they spill out in exactly the direction you hadn't counted on. And you have to start all over again. It's as if you are a hungry little beetle who has spent days trudging towards a pile of crumbs it has spied in the distance. It has made great growing plans for those crumbs. It has been thinking up crumb recipes…it will feed its whole family on these crumbs and there'll be crumb dinner parties for all its friends, enough crumbs for the whole of winter and no need to work, just a lot of sleeping in the slivers of sun, rocking on fat blades of grass and baking crumb casseroles. 'Oooh, what a lucky beetle I am,' thinks the beetle, and then, just as

lucky beetle   unlucky beetle

it's getting near, a human wipes away the whole pile of crumbs with a pink sponge Wettex and they're gone.

So the beetle must turn around and go back. It isn't lucky anymore. Now it's unlucky.

Before it saw the crumbs it was neither. Not lucky or unlucky. Just a beetle.

I wish I was just that, just a beetle with not a crumb in sight. Imagine if you could live without little hopes always budding. Imagine if you never looked ahead and never expected great things to happen, never hoped for a greater pile of crumbs than what you already had. No doubt about it, I was a dreamer, but worse, I was a greedy dreamer. I was a small, skinny girl dreaming giant, fat, champion dreams, I was dreaming piles of circus and love – but how do you stop it?

Maybe it's not about stopping, it's about choosing the right pile.

All I knew was that Kite must have been holding up my dream, and now it was sagging like a tent without its pole.

I wasn't ready to prop it up with new poles, so I let my mind sink into the withering, watery wretchedness that I knew was waiting for me. I knew I had to feel it. Just lie there and feel it.

Then I started to cry. Just a little bit. Just a few fat tears rolling down my face like little slugs.

plain beetle

Chapter 7

I must have cried myself to sleep because the next thing I remember is being woken up by a very strange guttural noise that moaned through the house and oozed under my door. Before I had a moment to figure out what it was, Barnaby flung himself into my room.

'You awake? Cedy? What the hell is that? Who's in Granny's room? Sounds like a cow, a mournful one.'

'Must be our new aunt. She's come from India.' I sat up. Stinky poked his nose in the door and I patted the bed, which signals to Stinky that he's allowed up. He runs and leaps and then takes his time to decide which ripple of doona is the best one for him to nestle into.

'What? Are you kidding?' Barnaby plonked himself on my bed too, and rubbed Stinky on the head.

'Nup. She's Dad's half-sister. Her name is Tirese. She can play drums and do headstands and Mum seems to like her a lot.'

'Dad's half-sister?' He frowned and thought about it a

while and tapped his foot on the floor. He always tapped quickly when he was figuring something. 'Yeah, right. I remember now, she was the one in India. Do you think she's okay? She sounds kind of woeful.'

'She's meditating.'

'They did mention her when I was in WA. What's she like? Look like Dad?' His sneakers kept thudding on the floor.

'She smiles like Dad, but actually she looks like me.' I found myself beaming for a minute, as if I'd just won something. I'd won myself a family resemblance. Suddenly I realised my new aunt must have somehow belonged to me; we had a thing we shared and that was special. Maybe I even liked her, even if she did make strange noises in the morning.

'You!' Barnaby laughed and I crawled out of bed and thumped him.

'Yeah, and I'm depressed, in case you want to know.'

He laughed again. And then, when I persisted with my depressed frown, he tried to be serious. He stopped tapping his foot.

'What's up?'

'The circus is over. Kite's moving to Albury to join the Flying Fruit Flies. His dad is going to be the new artistic director.'

'Albury!' he sucked the air between his teeth as if it was painful. 'Well, look at it this way, no one could last long in Albury. He'll be back. And in the meantime you can go train somewhere else and you'll be just as good as him when he comes back. Or you can learn something else. Like drums. We could do with a new drummer. Atticus is a big pain at the moment. He's just got no manners.'

Atticus is Ada's younger brother. The band is just Ada, Atticus and Barnaby. Both Atticus and Ada are dark and unusual. Their mum is a jazz singer and they live way out in Sunshine, and I don't think the sun shines any more in Sunshine than it does here in Brunswick, because Ada says Sunshine is a hole. Atticus has a long black fringe, which hides his eyes, and he never wipes it out of the way so he looks like a sheep dog. Ada has the same hair, only hers is very long and you can see her face. She's pretty, but she usually wears a tough expression by putting her mouth in a line and staring in a hot, accusing way, which makes you feel as though she might not like you. Neither Atticus or Ada have friends, though Barnaby says they're really bright, and Ada is reading *The Heart of Darkness*, and when there's no one else around they even laugh and make jokes. Ada sings, and the weird thing is she sings all sweet and ethereal, like an angel, even if the song is called Thanitos, which means hate in Latin. Mum and I aren't sure about Ada, but she's the first girl Barnaby has really liked. He's kind of crazy about her in fact. He says she's creative.

'Where were you last night?' I said.

'Rehearsal. Looks like the tour's going to happen. In fact we'll be doing Albury, on the way to Sydney.'

Their band is actually doing really well. They have a record company and a CD and they're called Badlands.

'Oh, so Badlands plays Albury. Great. That's just great.' Just what I needed. As my circus was dying, Barnaby's band was flying and somehow the dreaded Albury was in the middle of it. I guess I was also a little bit secretly proud, but I didn't want to say that. Kids at school thought I was cool because Barnaby was my brother and Barnaby was in Badlands. It was an easy way to get respect. But I wasn't cheating. I never asked for it. There's a song by Badlands on the radio. It's called 'I don't live in the same places' and I think it's about being different. But that song is how they got to be known. You couldn't say they're famous, because they're not popular. They're alternative, which means that mothers and tennis players and people with briefcases will never buy their CD. But still.

'Yeah well, Cedy, if you learned to drum in a month or two, you could get in on the act. Imagine that.' Barnaby laughed and I snorted.

'As if.' But some part of my brain had a wriggle going in it, and I got out of bed feeling a bit better than I did when I got in.

Chapter 8

This is how my thinking went as I walked towards school that morning.

Albury.

Boy, I hate that place. I mean, why would anyone start a circus way out there? Stupid.

Albury. Boy.

I'm going to kick that stone as far as I can.

Not a great kick. Never mind. More important things to mind about.

Like Albury.

Such a long way away from me. We drove through it once on the way to Sydney for a family holiday. It would probably take about four hours on a train to get there, and it's not exactly a ripping part of the country. Okay, let's not be rude about Albury because actually it's got a great raging river running through it, which is about ten times as wide as the Merri Creek and about ten times more exciting and scenic and swimmable, so there you go, that's a big plus. The problem with Albury is just that it's far away from me.

Now, some people might say that's exactly what's great about Albury; not its distance from me exactly because, let's face it, most people in the world don't even know who I am (though they will one day, once I'm infamous). For now, it has to be admitted, I don't even have an ant-sized amount of importance in the lives of the Albury-dwellers in general, but what they like about Albury is its distance from the city, which makes it a country town and not a major urban centre of much cultural activity and smog and stressed people honking. So in the end you have to just say, 'Oh well, horses for courses,' or whatever that saying is. My mum, for instance, would probably love Albury because she likes to think she's the earth mother of Brunswick, though she really isn't. Look at our backyard compared to Caramella's. Ours is neglected and flapping. Caramella's is all abundantly organised with beds of vegies and lines of fruit trees. But then again, Mum's a single mother and she has a lot of other stuff to do before she can even think about gardening. Mum and I simply couldn't live in Albury (and let's not even consider Barnaby, because he'd just laugh in a scoffing way at the idea). The reason we couldn't live in Albury is that Mum wouldn't have her friends there and, more importantly, I wouldn't have mine. I mean, who knows, Albury could even be a great place, and you could probably find a paddock for your horse, but what it doesn't

have is Caramella, Oscar, Ricci, Pablo and Robert, and all
the rest.

So that rules out Albury.

✿   ✿   ✿

What about learning the drums and getting in on the
Badlands tour? I couldn't possibly learn something that
required me to sit down and keep counting over and over,
and even if I could learn drums it would take me years and
years to be good enough. Plus Ada doesn't like me.

'Hey.' That voice just cut right through my thoughts and
plunged in somewhere else.

Kite, I said to myself as I stopped dead and then swivelled
around.

He was leaning up against the school gate, hands in
pockets, head slightly tilted. He looked sad and careless, as if
in secret communication with the sky. But when he moved
away from the gate and came towards me, he seemed to be
moving with a slow purpose and his eyes looked darker than
usual. I dropped my school bag to the ground and shoved it
between my feet. I stood still and tried to act steady.

'What are you doing here?' I said.

'Waiting for you.'

'For me?'

'Yeah.' He seemed to yield.

Right then, I admit it, a very superficial thought came
to my mind. I wished Marnie would walk through the gates

and see me standing there with Kite. Kite who was tall and leaning, with hair uncombed by wind, and arms that didn't try, and who stood there, shining and true and waiting for me.

Shining and true in my eyes, anyway.

I didn't say anything. He was leaving, after all. Suddenly he didn't look so shining and true. He looked like a deserter. I just looked at him as if I was Jesus Christ and he was Judas, the traitor.

'You're mad at me, aren't you?'

'Nope,' I lied. I looked up into the sky. Yellow leaves swirled through the grey air. The trees shook and waved their branches in the air, as if appalled, somehow. 'Well, maybe.' I corrected myself and frowned. Jesus Christ wouldn't have blamed anyone. 'See, I'm mad at the situation. Not at you, because you can't help it, but I'm mad that the circus will have to stop when we've just got it going.'

He glided closer. 'Cedar, it doesn't have to stop. You can keep it going.'

As if, I thought, but I maintained my fierce frown. He laughed at me because he could see right through my ferocity, and he knew he could have bent it out of shape with one smile.

'And think of the new tricks I'll bring back with me.' He made a little cheerful shoulder move, as though we were boxing and he'd just dodged a blow.

I nodded with obvious reluctance. As if, I thought again. As if he'd be coming back. Anyway, it wasn't just the circus

finishing. It was more than that. It was more selfish than
that. As I stood there in front of Kite I was suddenly aware
that some icky, lurking feeling was about to leap out of my
depths like a fish yanked out of the ocean by a hook. Some
feeling so icky and so bad-tasting that I'd been keeping it
under, keeping it simmering beneath the righteous display of
huffiness. But now, now that I was face-to-face with Kite,
that feeling was writhing and twisting like it had been
dropped in a bucket and it needed to breathe. It was making
me pale.

It was jealousy.

That's what it was.

Writhing and twisting.

I was jealous.

*   *   *

See, even worse than the fact that our circus was being
replaced by a better one was the fast encroaching and alarm-
ing probability that *I* would be replaced. Me. When it came
down to it, the thing that hurt the most was this: someone
else, some better, real acrobat would be doing the helicopter
with Kite. Okay, let's be honest, not just some other acrobat
but some other *girl* acrobat. To me that was unbearable.

'I can't imagine you'll be coming back to our circus,
Kite.' I kept pretending that this, this was what mattered
most. This, I was allowed to care about, because the circus
was important.

'Yeah, I will, I'll come back here. I won't live in Albury.'

I looked down. The world seemed like an odd, confusing place.

'I'll write to you,' he said.

I sighed, and then he sighed, and his voice went soft. 'Don't be mad, Cedy. I have to do this.' He turned his face away from me and looked out towards the trees, as if he was seeing into the distance, to the time when he would be in Albury and I would be here, at school. I looked too, and I felt as if I'd been hollowed out, as if a great empty space was about to swallow me. It made me feel lonely. And then I felt sad and I wanted him to take my hand again. But he didn't. He looked down at me as if he knew that I was hollow enough to break. The look landed so softly that it felt as if he had somehow touched me, even though he hadn't.

'When do you go?' I said.

'Friday.'

'That's in four days.'

'Yep. It's soon.'

'I'll be sad.' I said it. I just went and said it. It fell out of me in a pile of small broken up words – the truth. I felt like I'd just busted through a wall and come out in tatters. It didn't matter, though, because next thing I knew his arm looped out and pulled me in towards him and we hugged, just for an instant, and he looked down and said, 'I'll miss you, Cedar.' Then he turned around and walked up the street, arms swinging in a brilliant way.

Chapter 9

It wasn't the last time I saw him, but it was the last time I saw him alone.

Ruben organised a bit of a dinner party, mainly for the circus, but he also invited Mum and Barnaby and Ricci and Oscar's parents and Caramella's too. Aunt Squeezy came along, and so did Stinky, of course. So there were a lot of people, and there was a lot of commotion since Ricci was very excited because she never goes to dinner parties and she was squawking and pulling everyone on the nose.

Ruben had made a big lasagne, and Ricci brought along some spicy chicken dish with beans. We all squashed into the living room with plates on our knees, and I perched on the arm of a couch between Aunt Squeezy and Caramella's mother, who hardly speaks but keeps patting your knee and smiling. Kite was sitting on a cushion on the floor, and he spent most of the night speaking to Barnaby. I kept trying to hear what they were saying but could only make out bits, because if Mrs Zito wasn't passing me some bread or piling more beans on my plate, Ricci was screeching and yelling out and laughing at any old thing and making indelicate observations, like, 'Oooh Cedar, why the long face?' I just rolled my eyes and acted like a moody teenager, and Barnaby winked at me.

Aunt Squeezy elbowed me and whispered, 'Hey, he's a good sort, that Kite, isn't he?'

I said, 'He's okay.'

She said, when she was my age she was in love with a boy purely for his blue eyes and fragile smile. She said he wore hand-knitted jumpers and long pants, and he hung back in the playground and didn't play footy. But she could never speak to him because she was too shy, and then he left the school and she never saw him again. Now, she said, I'm all for courage. If you're scared of something it's a good sign you need to go towards the thing you're scared of.

'I'm not scared of things,' I said.

She laughed as if that was a very funny thing to say, but before I could ask why, Oscar made a commotion by knocking over a glass of wine on the carpet while waving his arm around and making some declaration. Ricci yelled for salt and Kite went to the kitchen to get some. When he came back, my mum stood up and said we should raise our glasses and toast Ruben and Kite. She said, 'To their new beginnings. Best of luck.' I looked down at the wine stain on the carpet, now covered in a tiny mountain of salt. Everyone

clapped and Ruben stood up and made a speech about The
Acrobrats, and he especially thanked me. Everyone looked at
me, which was the last thing I wanted. Kite didn't look at
me, though – he looked at his dad.

Ricci came and squeezed me to her chest and said, 'Chin
up, they'll be back, won't you, Ruben?'

Ruben said, ''Course we'll be back,' and he smiled at my
mum and she smiled quickly and then looked at the floor.
Kite shot a look in my direction; he simply raised his
eyebrows and grinned.

Oscar said, 'But only after Paris, after your world tour,
after the nights on the river.'

Everyone laughed at Oscar's poetry, but I noticed how
the mountain of salt was becoming pink at the base. As if it
was bleeding. As if it was trying very hard to do what it was
meant to do.

Had it all been done? I wondered, as Oscar's mum
brought out a passionfruit sponge cake. She's a librarian, and
librarians happen to be very good at cooking sponge cakes,
as far as I know, because I've met two and both cook sponge
cakes, so that's good odds there's a link. Boy, am I a sleuth.
But why was I wasting my time making links between
librarians and sponge cakes when I should have been lip-
reading the conversation between Kite and Barnaby? I could
tell they were really digging in on something and I was sure
I heard my name. I tried to watch, but Oscar's mum was
going round the room, pushing the plate of sliced-up cake

pic of librarian
passionfruit sponge
cake.

towards everyone, blocking my view. Was she in on it? Was
there something going on that I didn't know about?

When we left we all gave Kite and Ruben a goodbye
hug. There was a queue. It was like Pin the Tail on the
Donkey, and it happened so quickly I hardly had time to
take it in. When it came to my turn, Ruben took both my
hands and told me I was an angel and an inspiration.

'I want you to carry the torch. This is for you.' He
pressed a book into my hands. *The Tumbler's Manual.*

'Thanks, Ruben.' I felt quietened by the gift.

'Come and visit us any time. I really mean that. We see
you as one of the family.' He looked right in my eyes to
make sure, and then he gave me a big hug and I hugged him
back. Suddenly I felt terribly sad about Ruben leaving. I
hadn't even realised that he meant something to me. He was
important. His big, gentle way was something I loved
without even knowing it, not until it wasn't going to be
there. Maybe I even wished I was his child and that I could
always depend on him, and he could always show me how

to do something without trying too hard. I didn't say a word, though – I was feeling too emotional to speak.

Kite was leaning into the doorway. His arms were folded and he was laughing with Barnaby. His laugh tumbled out, and he moved with it, as if he was light, as if he could have floated up and lain in the sky, laughing. And I felt better just hearing it because it clattered in my head and loosened up all the hard thinking in there. I felt real. I felt like I didn't need to try and think of anything, not even a good thing to say. He must have known I was coming because even though he didn't look, even though he was still talking to Barnaby, his arm reached towards me like a wing and folded me in close. And I stood under his arm, tucked in by his side, just like a real girlfriend. And never had I felt happier. Never had I felt warmer. Never had I wanted to stay so still. And it had all happened as if it was the most natural thing in the world.

Before I had a chance to even know it, Barnaby was winking at me and saying goodbye and it was just us, just Kite and me and the small, pressed distance between us. Kite turned towards me with his unguarded eyes. While we hugged he whispered in my ear, 'I'll be back.' And I nodded but I didn't speak. I could tell then that it hadn't all been done and, more importantly, I could tell that he knew too. And with this, like a little hot coal in my heart, I turned away and walked.

And I swung my arms in a brilliant way.

✫   ✫   ✫

We all walked home together, except for Oscar and his family, because they don't live in our street. Mum and Ricci walked with Mr and Mrs Zito, and Aunt Squeezy walked with Barnaby. Caramella and I lagged behind.

The sky was black and clear, but in Melbourne the stars don't shine out because there's too much light coming from the city and the stars just can't compete. They look like smudged dots of white. But the houses have a golden light glowing through the windows, which makes you want to look inside. It makes it seem as if there are a lot of soft welcoming couches in the world; even if there aren't, it makes it seem as if there are. Still, I sighed a big sigh since I knew I wasn't going to see Kite again for a long time. Caramella said, 'Don't worry, you'll think of something. You always do.'

Do I? I wondered. I looked at Caramella trudging along, steadfast and solid and sweet, and I suddenly realised that somehow it wasn't just me who needed me to think; it was also Caramella, and maybe Oscar too. Maybe they were expecting me to think us out of this, or at least into something else. Boy, what a responsibility. I shivered and looked up into the sky as if it would have an answer, it being so much bigger than me. But if it answered I didn't hear, because instead my ears were filled with the faintly disturbing sound of a snigger and then a giggle. It didn't exactly surprise me, since we'd just walked past Harold Barton's house, but I'd been staring into the sky and not noticed who was sitting on the wall.

Not only Harold but also Marnie, Aileen Shelby and one or two other tall guys I'd never even seen before. A whole gang of them, smoking, sniggering and whispering.

'Night out with the family, Cedar? Paint the town red?' said Harold, now that he had my attention. Marnie and Aileen acted like this was a hilarious joke and started to smirk. Caramella sighed and looked at the ground. I folded my arms across my chest.

'Harold,' I said in an exasperated way, 'haven't you got a new act yet? Because we're really bored of your superior one.'

Harold snorted, pushed out his lower lip at me, and since he obviously couldn't think of a comeback he leaned over to whisper something to one of the tall guys.

'Who's your brother talking to, anyway?' said Marnie. 'He didn't even introduce us.' She had her special sneery girl voice on, which makes her sound like she's not quite real, like she's just saying some lines she learnt from a bad teen movie.

'Maybe he didn't notice you, Marnie,' I said, because if there's one thing Marnie puts a lot of energy into it's getting noticed. I walked off, dragging Caramella with me. I wasn't going to tell them who Aunt Squeezy was. Let them wonder, I thought.

'See ya, Zit-face,' yelled Harold, once we were a safe distance away.

He's such a coward. He just had to hurl one last witless insult so he could look as if he'd been victorious or something. But it kills me when he says something hurtful to Caramella because she has no confidence; she dies a little inside when he says stuff like that. Whereas I, I just get mad. I looked at her, but she was already tugging at my arm and pointing at something else.

'Hey, look at that,' she said.

A van had pulled up outside the Abutula's house and out of the van came three people: first a girl, then a woman and last a small boy. It appeared to be a mother and two children, but it was dark and they were on the opposite side of the street so it was hard to see them, and they seemed not to want to be seen. The girl was thin and taller than me and she turned away from us. Her younger brother, however, stood and faced us. He didn't smile; he just looked and stuck his finger in his mouth. The mother kept her face lowered, but glanced quickly at us and then ushered her children towards the house. Mr Abutula had picked up the suitcase and was leading the way.

'See,' said Caramella, triumphantly, 'something *is* going on there.'

'Sure is,' I said, and already I was getting ideas. The thing about the mother and her children was that you could tell they came from somewhere else. They weren't from here. They were different.

Chapter 10

The thing is, I understand what it's like to be different because I'm just slightly different myself. In some ways I'm exactly the same, of course. For instance, I've got skin and it hurts when someone pokes it. And the main way I'm exactly like everybody else alive and breathing and pooing is that I don't like it when I'm sad or lonely or angry – I much prefer to be excited. If I had it my way, I'd always be just about to do something lovely, like a cartwheel.

Also, if I had it my way, everyone, absolutely everyone, would love me. Not up-close, and not in the way the big guns like Jesus and Saint Francis of Assisi and Gough Whitlam were loved; not even as much as Cathy Freeman is loved for being a fast runner who doesn't show off and who carries the flag for Aborigines. I just want the people who know me to love me just for being me, in an everyday kind of way. They don't have to sing songs about it.

Aunt Squeezy says that doesn't make me any different from anyone else, because all people want to be loved, even if they wear safety pins in odd places. Even if they say mean things or forget to take a bath, they still want to be loved.

But I don't have it my way, and so some people don't love me at all. Like Harold Barton. He doesn't love me; he thinks I'm a no-hoper. And Marnie thinks I'm so uncool, absolutely in every way, and sometimes Barnaby thinks I'm a pain. And Kite can't be sure if he loves me or not, because he just went off and left.

But no one has it all their way. Aunt Squeezy says we think we're steering the ship, but really the ship is steering us, so we may as well let go of the wheel. You can't *make* people like you, you can only try to like people. Even Harold.

So, in that way I'm still exactly the same as everybody.

But I'm sure I'm different in some way. I feel as if I am. I told Aunt Squeezy that I was and she just looked at me with her owl eyes and grinned. We were in the kitchen, and she was cooking. She had a pale green scarf tied in her hair and she looked like an exotic bird, because of the way she hopped from one position to the next.

'Everyone thinks they're different.' She waved a wooden spoon at me and then dunked it in a pot. I was lurking and leaning in the doorway, not quite ready to go or stay. To tell you the truth it was beginning to bug me that she kept pointing out how I was just like everybody else.

I stood up straight and said, 'No, but I really am different. I'm slightly unusual. I'm not in the main swell, I'm in a puddle.'

'Oh, you mean you feel left out. You feel like you don't fit in.'

'No, I feel like I make my own puddle because I like it better there.'

'I know that feeling.' She sighed a big earth-moving sigh.

I was suspicious. I felt she was stealing my feelings. My unique feelings. She was flouncing round, tipping spices into a big pot of lentils and stealing my feelings. It was kind of great having her around because she cooked food all the time, and since Mum was always at work and too tired to cook, and Barnaby only knew how to make spaghetti with a can of tomatoes, and I only made cheese and tomato Brevilles, it was exciting to have someone making a big deal about meals. She even made porridge in the morning, with dates in it and grated apple and almonds on top. But, best of all, she was always up for a talk. And I mean a *real* talk. A chewing and burrowing and blazing-up kind of talk, not just a how-was-your-day kind of talk. She and I got to talking about real things. I'd never met someone who wanted to talk about life as much as I did; about the big stuff like love and difference and hope and lentils and the nervous system and bigotry. And if you don't know what that means (I didn't either), you should find out because there's a lot of it going round and I believe it's catchy, and if you get it you become very mean spirited, especially towards people who are different.

'But I've always been slightly unusual. Ask anyone. Mrs Duffel said it on my school report.' Mrs Duffel was my grade four teacher and she had red hair too, and she wore short dresses covered in swirly patterns. She was lovely.

Aunt Squeezy said, 'Oh Lord, Cedar, we're all slightly unusual.' And she giggled.

I bit my lip and sulked for a moment. I plonked myself down at the kitchen table as I could tell we were heading for a session. Sometimes she really got me thinking in ways I didn't want to have to be thinking.

'So who is *usual* then, if everybody is slightly unusual?' I was quite pleased with that bit of logic. I felt I had laid a very fine trap. In fact I was so pleased with the excellence of my trap that I forgot that my slightly unusual life was under siege, and I sat back and grinned.

Aunt Squeezy stopped moving for a minute.

'Hmmm. Maybe *you* can be. Then you'll be the only usual one and you'll be special, for your usualness. Imagine that?' She laughed. 'Cedar B. Hartley, the only person in the world who is usual.'

'I'd be an outcast!' I pronounced.

She laughed again but she didn't say anything, and I knew I was meant to do the thinking. Just as I got going she butted in.

'Oh, but really, don't you think it's the most perfectly beautiful thing in the world to discover the tiny singularities that are stitched into the seams of our souls?' She sat down opposite me and her eyes lit up as if she was seized by a great excitement. 'There's nothing more necessary and beautiful than the differences between us.' She gazed through

the window and her eyes flickered out. I knew her mind was
floating back to something else, something that made her
quiet, maybe the same something that had made her stay on
with us. When Mum had told her we'd love her to live with
us as long as she liked, Aunt Squeezy got tears in her eyes
and hugged my mum, and since then it just seemed as if
she'd always lived with us, even though it was only a month.
I knew it was a month because I was counting the days that
I hadn't heard from Kite. Every time the mail came I was
disappointed. I'd even tried to pretend to myself that I wasn't
expecting anything, but that didn't work.

So Aunt Squeezy was gazing out the window and I was
gazing inwards at my tiny singularities when Barnaby and
Ada walked in.

'What's going on, ladies?' said Barnaby. He had his arm
around Ada, but she didn't have her arm around him. She
leant into him and smiled at us, just a tiny smile.

'Cedar's trying to work out how she's unusual and I'm
cooking lentil soup. Are you two in for dinner?'

Barnaby looked at Ada, who shrugged. She never stayed
for dinner, so it was hard to read the shrug. Maybe it meant
she didn't care. I liked her long black hair, which went all
the way to her elbows and spread out like a curtain over her
red jumper. Somehow she always managed to look dramatic,
to look like tragedy and glamour.

'Maybe,' said Barnaby. 'We're just going to rehearse a few
songs in my room first.'

Typical, I thought. Non-committal. I hardly ever tried to talk to Ada. In some way she scared me. She didn't appear to love me at all, and that made me feel bad around her, so I didn't care if they weren't in for dinner anyway. Well, maybe I did. I liked it when everyone sat down together. It made me feel like we were a gang.

Of course I quizzed Barnaby on what he was talking about with Kite, but he claimed not to remember. I don't believe him, but I've had to give up because if there's anyone who can match my persistence with resistance it's Barnaby. I think it actually amuses him to beat me.

He ruffled my hair, even though that also annoys me, and as he was walking out he said, 'You were just born unusual, Cedy. You came out upside-down.'

'At least I didn't come out with a big mouth,' I yelled after them, and I think I heard Ada let out a little laugh. I was glad about that. I was glad she laughed because she sometimes seems to be made of glass instead of skin. But see, we all have skin and it hurts when you poke it. Even Ada. Even Harold and Marnie. Even that strange family that arrived in the night at the Abutulas. I was thinking about them, when I wasn't thinking about Kite, that is; when I wasn't 'moping', as Mum said, or limping around lovesick, as Barnaby said. I was thinking about that family and I didn't even know why. I started to figure that maybe I had to find out who they were and then I'd know why I was thinking about them.

But for once it wasn't me who worked it out.

Chapter 11

Actually, all of a sudden there was a lot of secret stuff going on around our house. It had something to do with Aunt Squeezy, I could tell that much, but I couldn't tell if Barnaby was in on it or not because he was also acting a bit weird. Or maybe he was acting a bit normal, which was weird because he's not normal; he's half wizard and half zebra. Not really. He's just like the bit of wood on a fence that juts out. But, lately, even he was quiet or in-place somehow.

picture of Barnaby
as a zebra

All I can say is there was an atmosphere of secret, muffled conversations, puzzled expressions, shut doors and empty late-night wine bottles growing in the recycle box. And there was a letter that arrived for Aunt Squeezy, and it came from Italy; a thin pale blue envelope covered in large stamps and elegant spindly lettering. I found it, of course, in the letterbox, where there should have been a letter from Kite. But there wasn't, only that exotic-looking thing and a gas bill. I slid it across the table towards Aunt Squeezy, hoping I might get to soak up some of her excitement, but she just opened her eyes in alarm, stared at it as if she didn't quite believe it was real and then, as if on autopilot, took it into the back garden. She didn't say a word, didn't emit one little squeak of excitement, and when she came back she just hovered for a moment with this stiff, thin smile, and then plunged into her bedroom.

After that there was a hushedness. She and Mum would be talking in the kitchen, and whenever I came into the room they'd stop their conversation and Mum would turn to me and say something to change the topic, like, 'Here's Cedar.' And I'd say, 'Yep, here I am,' and she'd say, 'Still moping?' and I'd say, 'Yep, still moping,' and then, after a significant pause, I'd say, 'What are you two talking about?' Of course I wanted all the pity I could get, especially now that something else was getting all the attention, but I also wanted to find out what was going on.

'I know how to stop you moping,' said Aunt Squeezy.

'Cedar likes moping. She likes the attention,' said Mum, somewhat cruelly, I thought. Where was all the sympathy going? Certainly not where it was needed. I rolled my eyes at Mum and, in order to prove her wrong, I faced Aunt

Squeezy like a puppy, eager and willing. She grinned and leaned forward.

'Volunteer work. You can come with me tomorrow, after school. They always need some help down at the Learning Network.'

'What?' I felt duped. I thought she was going to suggest a night at the movies, or a trip to the beach to try out some surfing, or at the very least a double choc Magnum and a video. I could see Mum was amused.

'What a great idea. If there's one way to stop feeling sorry for yourself, it's to stop thinking about yourself.'

'It might be more interesting,' added Aunt Squeezy, and she made a pleading face, as if she knew it was a long shot to convince a devastated, lovelorn teenager that someone else's troubles might be more interesting than her own. I knew they were trying to tell me that my 'poor me' act was worn out and overused and it was time to find a new act. But I can tell you, if I had a choice of new acts to choose from, volunteer wouldn't even get in on the top fifty.

'I don't think I'd make a good volunteer. What can I do? I can't even tie a knot.'

'You could just come and see. I bet once you came and met some of the people there you'd think of something you could do.' Aunt Squeezy shrugged and yawned. Her attention seemed to spiral inwards and she closed her eyes for a moment. Mum got up and patted her on the shoulder.

'Ginger tea?' she said. I sighed and slumped dramatically

on the table, as I could see I'd already lost their attention and
had to resort to desperate measures.

'All right, I'll do it, I'll be a volunteer. I'll come,' I declared.

'Good on you,' said Aunt Squeezy. 'We'll go tomorrow.'

Mum now had her attention on bills. She suddenly
turned around waving an envelope, looking like a young girl,
like a cheerleader.

'Look, it's a letter to me. From Ruben.'

'To you?' I wailed and leapt up to see. Surely it was a
mistake.

'Yes, to me.' She blushed and sunk into the chair. I
couldn't help frowning. Couldn't help thinking that this made
it even worse that Kite hadn't written, even more obvious
and inescapable and purposeful. And why would Ruben
write to my mum? I couldn't help wishing it was to ask for
permission to let me go and train in the circus too. Suddenly
I felt hopeful and watched her as she opened the letter.

A small folded square of paper fell out and landed on her
lap. She picked it up and squinted to read the writing, and then
a small smile began to dance on her face. She handed it to me.

'This one's for you, love.'

'For me?' I squealed. My heart started to thud almost
instantly. I knew who it was from. I could tell. I took it and
ran outside to be private. I sure didn't feel like anyone
watching me read.

'Well, well. There're a lot of letters coming in this week,'
said Aunt Squeezy as I left.

Chapter 12

Hi Cedar,

Remember me? Or has some other acrobat swung out of a tree?

I've been thinking of you, but I never know what to write and say, but now there's going to be an audition up here in two months (December 5) and since I reckon you should come up for it, that seems like something to write about.

Anyway, you'd like it here. Maybe not Albury, but the circus, it's great. You should see the equipment. Dad's doing a good job.

I don't know what to tell you.

Days wear on.

It's getting warmer.

I've got blisters (doing some flying trapeze).

You'd like the trees here. So would Stinky.

How're Oscar and Caramella?

Are you attracting any attention with your bat pole positions?

Be good and come up.

Love Kite.

I read it through about seven times before I stopped to
think about it. I wondered why he set it out like that. So it
would take up more room and look longer, probably. I have
to admit, I wasn't happy with how short it was. Not a lot of
thought had gone into it…no endless hours lying in bed,
pencil in mouth, thinking about how to put this and how to
express that. Plus there was no kiss at the end, no I miss you.
There was a lot that wasn't in it, let's face it. But then again,
there are things you have to take into account, like for
instance, he's a boy, and boys don't give too much away and,
as I once said before, it becomes a girl's job to learn how to
read things that aren't said. The problem with this is that if
you happen to be a girl with an overactive imagination you
can read a whole lot of extra stuff into everything, because
you tend to read things with a certain imaginative vigour
and a kind of leap-happy attention that jumps off and runs
further and further until you are making quite faraway
assumptions and thinking of desperate implications…

Like for instance, just say Marnie is your friend (*God help
you*), and if one day she just happens to not say hello to you
(*because actually she's busy focusing her attention on getting Angus
Bennett's attention*), you might just decide that means suddenly
she hates you (*wrong*) and you get to wondering what on
earth you did to make her hate you *(nothing)*. Was it because
you were absolutely committing a glaring and embarrassing
fashion blunder by wearing your brother's hand-me-down
King Gees? Because Marnie for sure wouldn't abide that.

(*True, but this was not noticed because she was too busy flirting with Angus Bennett.*) So then you begin to believe that really you must be a worthless person because you make fashion blunders. (*If you'd been thinking, instead of imagining, you'd have known that fashion victims are the ones to be pitied, not us fashion crime-committers.*) So you decide the only thing that will redeem you is the purchase of a brand new pink zip-up parka. (*What a big waste of money, and lucky for me I don't even like pink parkas, anyway.*)

Fortunately, I'm already disliked by Marnie, and my best friend Caramella is an artist and not a snob, so I haven't had to go out and buy a pink parka, but still, I do tend to run away with my interpretation of events.

Here's how I read the letter:

Hi Cedar,

Hopefully he wanted to say, My dear Cedar, but that sounds too much like an old gent from last century, so he opted for a more casual version of greeting.

Remember me?

As if I'd have forgotten him. He knows very well I'll never forget him even if I don't hear from him ever again. Obviously he's sarcastically overcompensating for extreme guilt he feels from not having written sooner.

Or has some other acrobat swung out of a tree?

Hmmm. Can I possibly detect a note of jealousy? Hope so.

I've been thinking of you

Obviously not quite enough to make you write sooner.

but I never know what to write and say,

Why not? Is there something you can't tell me? Do you have a new girlfriend? Is she an absolutely brilliant acrobat with interesting views on life and big boobs?

but now there's going to be an audition up here in two months (December 5) and since I reckon you should come up for it, that seems like something to write about.

Yes, that's a safe thing to write about. As if my mum will let me go, anyway.

Anyway, you'd like it here. Maybe not Albury, but the circus, it's great. You should see the equipment. Dad's doing a good job.

Blah blah, boring boring, reveals nothing. Who cares about equipment? What about the other acrobats? Why don't you tell me about them?

I don't know what to tell you.

You sure don't.

Days wear on.

You're really struggling.

It's getting warmer.

Obviously. It usually does.

I've got blisters (doing some flying trapeze).

Am I meant to feel sorry for you?

You'd like the trees here. So would Stinky.

Nice of you to think of us, actually.

How're Oscar and Caramella?

Being polite now, or are you actually missing the old Acrobrats and their hotchpotch magic?

Are you attracting any attention with your bat pole positions?

Hmmm. Could possibly be a second but well-disguised note of jealousy. But more likely feeling guilty about attracting a bit of attention himself and is trying to deflect guilt.

Be good and come up.

Knows I can't come, but wants to act like he wants me to anyway.

Love Kite.

If he really meant 'love', why didn't he add a kiss or two?

✿   ✿   ✿

'He could be too shy,' says Aunt Squeezy. 'Men often are.'

I've shown her the letter because she has forced me to. I'd finally returned to the kitchen after my private half hour of interpreting on the back step. I'd considered burying myself in my bedroom but decided a bit of sympathy was in order so I'd gone and sighed loudly in the kitchen instead.

Aunt Squeezy is standing at the bench chopping an onion. She responds appropriately to my sigh by asking me what's wrong.

'Kite doesn't love me,' I declare and sink into a chair. Aunt Squeezy stops chopping, wipes her eyes with the back of her hand and faces me.

'Did he say that, Cedar? Did he say he didn't love you?' She puts the knife down and tries to puff at a red curl that is hanging over her eye, but it just floats up and then lies down again.

'He didn't need to, I could just tell by his letter.' I lift the letter feebly, but I look away from it, as if the sight of the offending piece of evidence is almost too much to bear. She sighs, wipes her hands on her jeans, tucks her hair behind her ear and comes towards me.

'Let me see, what makes you think that? I'll bet you're reading things into it.'

I roll my eyes and thrust the letter at her. She only reads it through once and then immediately tilts her head to one side and stares at me like I'm a dumbo.

'Are you mad? He's asking you to go up there and you're claiming he doesn't love you. Why on earth would he suggest you audition if he didn't want you to be in the circus?'

'He knows I won't be allowed to audition. Mum wouldn't let me.'

At this she tilts her head the other way and again she reminds me of a bird. She considers for a minute, puts her hand to her mouth and stares upward. Then she sits down opposite me and in a slightly conspiratorial way she says, 'Listen Cedar, where there's a will there's a way, and if it's really, really what you want to do then you will find a way. But first you have to think about it and make sure it's really, really what you want.'

I nod and then I say, 'But why didn't he put a kiss at the end?'

And that's when she stands up, goes back to chopping and says, 'He could be too shy. Men often are.'

'Men?' I say.

'Men and boys. They're similar.'

'Did Ruben write kisses on Mum's letter?'

'You'll have to ask her that, Cedar.'

'Yeah, right,' I say as I slide off the chair and skulk off towards my own room for some extra pondering. I wonder if she's right about Kite just being too shy. I must be convinced (easily done when you want to be) because, before I can stop it, I'm already turning my mind to something else. Do I really, really want to do the audition?

How to write a kiss

x x x x x x x x — little pecks

X — smooch

⊗ — kiss and hug together

xo X⊗ ⊗ X xxx ⃝ ox — making out

Chapter 13

Of course that night I ring Caramella, read her the letter and ask her opinion. She agrees with Aunt Squeezy that there's no sure sign that Kite has another girlfriend, and says I'm definitely over-interpreting, especially since the small hints of jealousy *are* there. But she's not sure about the audition.

'For one thing, what's the point, because your mum is never going to let you live in Albury,' she says.

'I know, but maybe if I did the audition and got in, she might be so proud of me she'd change her mind. Anyway, at least it would be a good excuse to go up there and visit, even if I don't get in.'

'Scary, though, doing stuff in front of people. All those kids up there, they'd be really good.'

'True, but you can't let fear get in your way, can you?'

'*I* can.'

'Yeah, but remember, you were scared of joining our circus, but once you joined you liked it.' At this she pauses to consider.

'Yeah, but that's different.'

'Why?'

'Because that was friendly; the Albury circus is serious.'

'Still…' I say. And then I don't know what else to say.

Later, I ask Barnaby. I don't show him the letter, because boys don't bother with interpreting. I just saunter into his room and hang in the doorway expectantly. He is lying on his bed, propped up by pillows, with headphones on, foot tapping. When he sees me, and when he sees I mean business, he pulls his headphones off and leans over to hit the pause button.

'What's up?' he says.

'There's going to be an audition for the Flying Fruit Fly Circus in Albury in December, and Kite thinks I should try out.'

'Does he?'

'Yep, he does.'

'What about you? Do you reckon you should?'

'I think so. Be pretty cool to be in a real circus, don't you think?'

He heaves himself up into a sitting position and screws his face up a bit, as if in a deep think. 'You're already in a real circus. With Oscar and Caramella. Remember?'

'Yeah, but I mean really real. I can't exactly be learning new tricks with Oscar and Caramella.'

'If tricks are what you want to learn, you can go do a class, can't you?' He's looking up at me again, but he isn't smiling, he isn't enthusing; in fact he seems confused, or disappointed, I'm not sure which.

I frown. I would have thought Barnaby of all people –
Barnaby who runs away from school and hitchhikes across
the desert to the other side of the country, and who never
obeys the rules and always does exactly what is interesting to
him, despite what people think – I would have thought he'd
be the one to say, Go! Go follow your dream.

'What's your problem, Barn? Why don't you want me to
go? How come it's okay for you to run off when you like
but not for me?'

He laughs as his palms fly in the air, as if he just
accidentally touched something too hot. 'Hey, it's your life,
Cedy, you decide. I just reckon you're already in a really cool
circus. I reckon it's the coolest circus I ever saw.'

'Hmph,' I say as I perform a stylish swivel and leave him
to his rock'n'roll. I go brush my teeth and then hop into
bed, and this is what I think.

Barnaby is just saying that 'cause he's jealous of me possibly
becoming a real circus pro. He just wants me to stay here, stay
small-time. I try to imagine what it would be like to be in a
real circus. I see myself in costumes, doing startling things on
a trapeze, but when I fall asleep I dream instead that a polar
bear is weeing on me, and Oscar is there but he doesn't help.

picture of a polar bear
who needs a wee.

Chapter 14

The next day I only just manage to get through school without getting caught doing some very glorious circus daydreaming. And then when I get home Aunt Squeezy is ready and waiting to whip me off to volunteering. I was hoping she might have forgotten or let me off because, after all, it was in my hour of weakness, before the letter arrived, that I'd been persuaded to do it. But she hasn't forgotten and she isn't letting me off.

On the way there we see Oscar in the distance. He's unmistakeable because of the slow, leaning way he drags his body along. He's ahead of us, edging down the street carrying a white plastic bag stuffed with something so that it's bulging out and lumpy. I yell out to him and he turns, raises his arm slowly and waits for us to catch up. I tell him about my weeing polar bear dream and he likes it. He doesn't seem to care that he didn't help me in the dream; he's too amused at the thought of a polar bear weeing on me.

'Did he wee on your head?' he asks.

'I can't remember where he weed,' I say and then, not wanting everyone to linger on the image, I change the topic. 'What's in the bag?'

'Pieces of blue.' His eyes remain blank and wide, even though he has said an odd thing.

'Pieces of blue?' says Aunt Squeezy. 'What are they for?'

Oscar opens the bag and pulls out a cut up bit of blue T-shirt. He holds it up as if it's an amazing thing.

'I'm going to wrap some rocks in blue. The ones that come down the hill, by the bridge. A blue stream of rocks.' He pronounces this slowly and then tucks the blue piece back in with the others.

'Wow, a blue stream of rocks,' says Aunt Squeezy. 'Oscar, it's like concrete poetry!'

'You must have been collecting them for a while?' I say.

'Yes, quite a while.' He looks ahead, and his head is wobbling and his eyes look as if they are searching, doing a big internal search for the right information. But he's quiet. Then he stops walking and looks at me. 'Since the circus stopped,' he says.

I take a deep breath and I stop too.

'Since Kite left,' I say, but I'm not looking back at Oscar, because I can't. And after that all three of us walk to the end of the street in silence and that's where we part, Oscar wobbling off to the creek with his pieces of blue and us waiting for the tram to take me into the world of volunteering.

Aunt Squeezy doesn't say anything about Oscar and the circus. She probably wants to keep me on-side, since I'm already a reluctant passenger. She's chattering on instead about my new job as a volunteer, but my mind isn't really on the job, it's on Oscar, all alone, sitting on a cliff, wrapping rocks in scraps of blue. I hardly take in what she's saying.

So I'm surprised when we arrive because it isn't at all what I expected. For one thing, the place we enter isn't a building amidst buildings, it's an old brick kindergarten on Napier Street. And also, it doesn't have the atmosphere of an office. It's not one bit quiet or organised or formal; it's more like a mad boarding house, only no one there's mad, they're just kind of comfortable and loud. Well, Eliza is. You can tell instantly that she's the main one; she's the boss, though she seems more like the head of a family. She's standing, large and smiling, all bosom and blonde curls, a sheet of paper in one hand, the other hand waving around, leading her attention from one thing to another: from Maude, a small neat woman in a green suit, who manages the office and is trying to fix up someone's dentist appointment; and then to the man who has come to fix the leak upstairs; and then back to Maude, who has someone on the phone who can't speak English well; and then to a young man with dark hair who appears to have no idea what's going on. She gathers him close, and gives him a huge grin and says to us (we're loitering in the hall, apparently waiting for her attention to fall on us), 'Oh, Tirese, this is Farid. He's from Afghanistan.

We're his new family. Have you seen Inisiya? We need her to translate.'

'I'll go check the computer club. This is Cedar, my niece, she's come to help,' says Aunt Squeezy, pushing me forward.

I immediately feel ashamed of my very small and self-centred life in front of Eliza, who has in one blow revealed herself to me as some huge-hearted, masterful conductor of this international orchestra of other people's needs. But at the same time I can tell she doesn't care how small my world or anyone's world is. She grins at me, just as she grins at anyone, and puts her hand gently on my shoulder.

'Good. Can you use a computer?' She waves her hand in the air, before I can answer. 'Doesn't matter, as long as you can speak English you can help just by getting them to practise their English. Why don't you go with your aunt to the computer club?' Again she can't even wait for me to speak because Maude has rushed up to us with something for Eliza to sign, and two more men enter with an older woman. Eliza excuses herself and swoops Farid off with her to greet them. I look at Aunt Squeezy, who says, 'Welcome to the Fitzroy Learning Network,' and leads me up the hallway towards another room.

'What *is* this place?' I say.

'Well, as far as I can make out, it was started as a kind of community centre that was set up to help women return to work by teaching them work skills. But, ever since the refugee crisis, it's had to adapt and become a place for helping refugees.' She stops and looks at me inquiringly, probably because she has already explained this to me on the way here but I was distracted then.

'How did that happen?' I say.

'Because the housing commission flats, where a lot of refugees live, are just up the road and there was a sign out the front of the centre saying free English classes. Apparently, a man from Afghanistan turned up one day and asked about the class and ever since the place has been flooded with all kinds of refugees who need to learn English, and how to use computers, even just how to catch trams, deal with the unemployment office, all that.'

'Wow.'

'But, even more importantly, from what I can see, what the centre really provides is a base, a place the refugees can come to and join in, feel connected, supported.'

I didn't know much about refugees, only that they came on boats because the countries they lived in were making life unbearable for them and they needed to live somewhere else. But Australia hadn't treated them well. They'd been made to stay in detention centres.

'Where are they from?' I ask, but before she can answer we've opened the door to a large room buzzing with voices. There's computers along the wall, and a large table in the middle, and hanging around everywhere are all kinds of kids. It's a bit like a classroom without a class going on, so instead of doing something dull, like maths, everyone is having fun.

There's two giggling girls in the corner taking photos of each other and then printing them up. One boy rushes over to the teacher, beaming. He's done a silly portrait of her. She laughs at him just as if she's one of the kids. Then she leans over a quiet boy and helps him colour something on the computer. This boy is the only one who doesn't look excited or interested, even though he's somehow focused and determined. I feel a bit sad, watching him, because he doesn't seem to care.

I'm standing there, shyly watching, because I can see straightaway that I'm the odd one out. I hadn't expected kids. Kids can be scarier than adults, because they're not polite; they say exactly what they think. So I'm not sure what to do.

I'd heard people talk about refugees, but I never had a picture in my mind that went with the word 'refugee'. So it was a word without a face; a word that got talked about and dealt with by other people. But once a word gets a body and a face that speaks, then it begins to be real to you and you begin to have feelings for it. Once I saw those kids, leaning over the table and helping each other out and laughing, I understood that word with my heart, not just my head, and it made me see that the closer you get to something the more it will mean to you, and then the more it will matter to you, and then the larger your life will become for having to reach out like a big embracing arm to hold it all.

I'm watching a tiny girl whose hair coils in little fuzzy knots on her head. When I smile at her she laughs and then runs away, and I laugh too.

'Come and meet Inisiya, she's about your age,' says Aunt Squeezy, pulling me towards the corner where a girl sits at the computer. Inisiya's dressed in jeans and a green zip-up sloppy-jo, and her long black shiny hair is tied back in a ponytail. I feel shy and wonder if she really wants to meet me, but Aunt Squeezy is already talking to her.

'Inisiya, Eliza needs you to translate. And I want to introduce you to my niece, Cedar. Inisiya's from Afghanistan.'

Inisiya pushes her chair back and turns around. She has large dark eyes which blink as she smiles at us. I recognise her immediately. She's the skinny girl who got out of the Abutula's van. I don't know if she recognises me. She simply says, 'Hi.' Then I say, 'Hi.' She stands up and asks Aunt Squeezy if Eliza needs her now, and then she wanders out to help. But I know then and there that we must have been meant to meet, and that I will find a way to talk to her. Already I can't wait to tell Caramella.

Chapter 15

When Mum comes home that night, she plonks herself down on the couch next to me. I'm watching *The Simpsons*, but it's a repeat so I don't mind her interrupting. At first it seems she has come in to talk about volunteering.

'So, how was the Learning Network? Did you enjoy it?'

'I did, actually.' I have to admit it, even though I hate to let her know that she was right about it being good for me. But I don't give her too much. She presses me for more, of course.

'Well, tell me, what did you do?'

'Oh, mainly I was just meant to talk to kids who need help with their English.'

'Ah,' she says, and by the look on her face I can tell her attention is drifting. I wonder then if this could be the right moment to bring up the audition. You have to pick the absolute optimum moment when asking for something that you know is going to be a very enormous ask. If you ask too early, it's like opening the oven door on a cake and

making it sag. I decide first to enthuse a bit about my new
position in the world as a volunteer; puff up the moment
with examples of me as her wonderful, deserving child.

'I met this great little boy called Sali from Sudan in
Africa. He has the most beautiful laugh. His dad is driving
cabs here. Also, there's this older boy who has no bottom
teeth, because he comes from a tribe where all teenage boys
have their teeth removed to prove they can bear pain and
become a man. Now Eliza is trying to organise a dentist to
replace them because here he feels self-conscious.'

'Oh God, I can imagine.'

'But guess who else I met?' I take her foot and remove
her shoe.

'Who?'

'The girl who Mr Abutula brought here with her mum
and brother. We saw them arriving, remember? The night
Kite left.' I'm massaging her foot and she is closing her eyes
slightly.

'Oh yes, I remember. What was she like?'

'Well I haven't really spoken to her yet, but I will next
time.'

'So you're going back again?' She smiles as if I'm an
angel. So I'm almost ready to land it on her.

'Yep. I'm going back next week.'

Silence for a while.

'Mum?'

'Mmm.'

'Kite asked me to go do an audition for the Flying Fruit Flies.' There, I said it. It's landed.

First she sighs (bad sign). I let go of her foot and she shifts a bit on the couch. She turns to face me.

'Cedar, it's wonderful he asked you. He and Ruben must have a lot of faith in your abilities. But you know we can't move to Albury. I have my job here. Can't you join a circus here, love? Or wait until you're a bit older and clearer that circus is really what you want to do? You're still so young.' She pats my leg and sighs again.

I know she doesn't like to disappoint me, and I experience a tiny second of understanding for her, but then I quickly move on to the more important issue of me. Why does everyone think I'm still too young to know what I want? Anyway, how can I know what I want until I try it out?

'I'm not too young to know what I love doing the most.' I look at her pleadingly, even though I know it's useless. She looks back at me with a look so full of sympathy and sadness that again I almost feel bad for making her feel bad about making me feel bad.

'How much do you think this is really about the circus and how much is it because you like Kite and you want to do what he's doing?'

'It's about the circus.' I'm looking at my hands, which are squirming on my lap. I'd hate anyone to think I'd do something just for the sake of a boy, and not because I wanted to do it myself. I'd even hate myself to think that, so I deny it out loud, straight away, and then I try very hard to believe it. My hands are still squirming. Mum says nothing. And then slowly it seems that we're both watching *The Simpsons* again, though I'm not concentrating as I am trying very hard to banish that thought and I'm not sure I'm succeeding. Would I want to go to Albury if Kite wasn't there? Yes or no? I try to think of something else. After a while Mum starts up again.

'Cedar?'

'Yes.' I keep staring at the telly.

'I know this might not be a good time, but there's something I want to talk about with you.'

'What?' I'm grumpy now. Why doesn't she choose her moments better, like I do? I always create the right time by giving foot massages. But she's not reaching for my stiff old neglected foot.

'It's about all the secret stuff that's been going on around here.'

'Oh, that.' I'm a bit more interested now, so I turn away from the telly.

'It's about Tirese.'

'What about her?'

'Well, she's pregnant.'

'Oh,' I say. And then I say, 'Wow!' and then I say, 'But I didn't even know she had a boyfriend.'

'She doesn't.' Mum looks at me as if she's working out

whether I'm really old enough to understand this. I strike a serious pose, tilt my head to the side, just like Aunt Squeezy does when she's considering. It seems to work. Mum explains. 'Well, she had one, obviously, while she was in India. She was studying yoga at some yoga centre, and she met a man there from Italy who became her boyfriend. He had to go back to Italy, and then she came here and discovered she was pregnant. So she wrote to him. He wrote back and told her that he had a wife and children already.'

'And hadn't he told her that before, while he was her boyfriend?'

'No.' Mum shakes her head disapprovingly.

'So he's a cad?' I say, and she laughs.

'Maybe – we don't really know. We all make mistakes, especially with affairs of the heart. It's easy to fall in love when you're on holiday, even if you shouldn't.'

'Is Aunt Squeezy sad?'

'Well, she's been confused, but she's decided to have the baby anyway, and that's why I thought she could stay here with us, because it's very hard to look after a baby on your own.'

'Like you had to with us?' I say. She nods and lowers her eyes.

'Kind of like that.' It always makes her sad when she thinks of our dad. But after a moment she looks up again and grabs my hand. 'Anyway, Cedy, how do you feel about it? How do feel about Tirese living here while she has her baby? I mean, it's okay with me as long as it's okay with you and Barnaby.'

'It's fine by me. It's great. You know me. I always want there to be a big family. I'd love there to be a baby here too. Does Barnaby know?'

'Not yet.'

'Really?'

I felt great. I grinned a big smug grin just because I knew something that Barnaby didn't know. I was in on the secret and he wasn't. For a moment I was so puffed up I almost forgot the life disaster that Mum had just inflicted upon me. But then I remembered it again and I decided to huff off over to Caramella's, just so Mum knew it meant a lot to me. Maybe she'd even reconsider.

Chapter 16

'I doubt it,' said Caramella. 'She won't reconsider. There's no way your mum could move to Albury. How would she work there?'

Caramella can be so practical. I stared at my chocolate macaroon gloomily. I knew she was right, but sometimes I just want her to play along with my dreams, or at least accompany me into the drama and tragedy of it all.

'Anyway, guess what?' I decided to change the topic.

Caramella never guesses, so I carried on. 'I did some superb sleuthing today. Kind of incidental sleuthing, but still.'

'What?' she said. She wasn't really looking at me, she was fiddling with the packet of biscuits. I wasn't sure, but suddenly I suspected she was upset about something.

'Are you okay?'

'Yeah,' she said, still not looking. 'Tell me what you discovered.'

'I met that girl who got out of the Abutula's van. She's from Afghanistan.'

'Oh. How did you meet her?'

'At the place where Aunt Squeezy volunteers.'

There was definitely something wrong. Where was the excitement? 'Caramella, tell me what's wrong. I know something's wrong.' I pulled the biscuits away from her.

'It's nothing.'

'No, it's something. Tell me. Have I done something?'

'No, you haven't done anything. That's the problem.' She looked up at me for the first time since the conversation began, her short bunched pigtails dangling above her shoulders as she hunched over the table and squeezed her plump little hands into a knot.

'What do you mean?' I said it quietly and gently. I could tell she was struggling to explain. She looked down again and bit at her lip.

'It's just, remember how when Kite left the circus you went on and on about him not caring about us and our circus? Well, now it seems you want to do exactly the same thing. You just want to leave and be a star and you don't seem to care about what happens to us.' She shrugged and pushed her lip out and looked at me like I was a traitor. I blushed and took a deep breath.

'No,' I said, shaking my head. 'It's not like that. I do care, of course I care…it's just…It's just, God, I just don't know how or what to do with us, with our circus.'

'Have you tried?'

Before I could answer, Mrs Zito waddled into the

kitchen, pinched my cheeks and asked me if I wanted to stay
for dinner. I was blushing because somewhere deep inside I
felt guilty and I didn't feel I could stay for dinner, so I stood
up and said thank you but Mum was expecting me home
for dinner. I smiled at Caramella and said I'd see her
tomorrow. She nodded feebly and I felt like a skunk as I left.
I felt like I was scurrying off and leaving a bad smell in the
air between us, because I couldn't face it, I couldn't work
out how to clean up the smell. Maybe Caramella was right.
But I couldn't figure it out on the spot. I knew there was a
bit of thinking to do but I had to go do it before I could
know what was what.

Chapter 17

I lie on my bed and stare up at the ceiling, because ceiling-gazing always brings on my loftiest thoughts. Stinky hops up on the bed with me, as he can tell I'm in for a stint.

This is how it seems to me: all of a sudden there are a few too many circuses and a few too many people pulling me in different directions. I feel as if I'm swimming down a river and on one side of the bank is the Flying Fruit Fly Circus, with Kite and Ruben and lights and proper equipment and my potential waiting, and on the other side there's Oscar, sitting alone with his pieces of blue; and there's Caramella, eating chocolate macaroons with her hands in a knot; and then there's Mum, who is trying to tie me to the shore; and then Aunt Squeezy on the banks with her pregnant belly, cutting the rope and calling out, 'Follow your dream'; and Barnaby in a boat, strumming his guitar singing, 'Oh I'm following mine.'

What do I really, really want? Seems like such a simple question. And if you answer it with your heart, you want whatever it is that makes your heart leap and brim and bound forward. If I listen to my heart I would be running away to audition for the Flying Fruit Flies. But then if my mind steps in (and it usually does), thinking happens, and once you start thinking everything gets complex and confusing and bigger than you. For instance, I start wondering, is my longing to join the circus for Kite or for me? And then I get to wondering about The Acrobrats. Aren't they my friends, my true friends, and isn't that more important than anything? Isn't that the right thing to do, to stay and hold the fort? And shouldn't I want to do the right thing? Because then I'll be a better person, a compassionate person like Eliza and the Buddhists.

But will I be boring? Even resentful?

Here, something else joins the battle, and this is a part of me that must come from my past life as an ancient Greek philosopher, because it takes an impossibly broad view. It asks, even if I do know that I should do the right thing, how do I know that what I think is right *is* in fact right? For instance, who's to say that to follow your heart or to live your dream is not the right thing, while trying to be a good person might just be like trying to wear something fashionable, even if it isn't you, even if it's high heels and you've got a back ache, or if it's a pink parka and you're allergic to synthetics? I mean, maybe I'm just not meant to be good. Maybe I'd come out in hives if I was good! Maybe the whole point is to find out not what you should do, but what you're meant for.

Of course, what I'm *meant* for is cartwheels and thoughts, but what I *want* is for everything, every person and reason and beat of my heart, to hop over to the same side – to the Flying Fruit Flies' side, because then it would be easy. But, as all good former Greek philosophers know, life doesn't come in easy packages. It's meant to be difficult. Otherwise you wouldn't have to think and wonder and make mistakes and learn, and then you'd really be boring.

Here's what I think:

All interesting people make mistakes.

All interesting people get themselves into a pickle at some stage, and then they have to figure out how to get out of it.

And it's the getting in and out of
pickles that gives you character.

picture of a small
person in a pickle

But was I getting anywhere with my pickle or was I just stewing in it?

I decide to write back to Kite. Until I can make a decision, I need to keep my options open.

Hi Kite,

Use the same greeting as he used – keep it equal.

Thanks for writing.

Resist temptation to get mad that it took him a while.

I was beginning to think you might have injured your hand.

Still, must let him know that it took a while.

All those trapeze blisters, I guess?

Dig it in a little.

My hands are softer than ever,

Dig it in even more, but in a surreptitious way.

but I have a new aunty who has come to stay and she is pregnant.

Just so he doesn't think my whole world stopped when he left.

Haven't been doing any hedge walking or bat pole positions.

Still must gather some sympathy.

But maybe I should start if I am going to audition?

If you show me that you care, then I will practise.

What would I have to do?

Don't let on yet that Mum has said no – must keep the option alive somehow…

Do you think I would have a chance?

Come on, Kite, tell me how good I am and how quickly I learn.

Aren't the others you train with really, really good?

Opportunity for him to let slip information about the other girls, the ones who are better than me.

I'm sure Stinky would like the trees. Oscar is making pieces of blue to wrap rocks in. Caramella is sad that there is no more circus here.

This is the ruin you have left in your wake.

I am trying to find a way to get The Acrobrats going again.

But see what a good person I am, see how I am a hero. (Hide the fact that I have tried nothing and collapsed entirely.)

Anyway, fly hard, Kite, and stay warm. Love Cedar.

What I really want to say is don't forget me, but you simply can't ask that, so instead I must act nonchalant.

X

Add a kiss. Recklessly.

PS Say hi to Ruben.

Quickly deflect attention from kiss.

Then I write a letter to Caramella:

Dear Caramella,

I understand how you feel and I want you to know that I am sorry for making you feel that way. (True.) I definitely don't plan to desert you. Both circuses are really important to me and I want to find a way to have both in my life. (Obviously impossible, but it's what I want.) I really want to learn more acrobatics with the Flying Fruit Fly Circus but I am also completely committed to our circus, because it's ours, and because we made it ours. (Well said, I think.) Anyway, I plan to do some thinking about our circus and see what we can come up with to keep it going, because now you've made me think about it I realise that I do miss it.

See you soon?

Your friend, Cedar

Then I write a short note to Aunt Squeezy:

Dear Aunt Squeezy,

Mum told me you've pregnant. I think that's great. Just wanted to tell you that. I hope you have a redhead baby!

Chapter 18

The next day is Saturday, and I have to say I don't feel great. I feel diluted, like once I'd been a strong colour and now I'd gone pale and insipid. Because I haven't been concentrating, I've been spreading out and trickling and not pouring my full undiluted glory into anything. One moment I'm thinking about The Acrobrats and Caramella and Oscar, and the next I'm wondering how can I go do that audition, and then I'm thinking that I'm not getting anywhere with either of them because they both seem to cancel each other out.

So I decide to take action. First, Stinky and I go to Caramella's and slip the letter under her door. Unfortunately, Ricci is on the prowl.

'Hey, why don't you just go in? They're home,' she shrieks. She's squinting at me suspiciously, nosing the air like she might catch a whiff of something.

'Because I just want to leave a letter,' I say.

'You like my new shoes?' she cries, obviously more interested in her shoes than in my letter. They're orange slip-on sneakers. She points her foot at me.

'They're great. Where'd you get 'em?' I'm relieved she isn't quizzing me, but just to make sure I keep her on the shoe topic.

'Savers, of course. You should see. They've anything you want there.'

'How about a new circus trainer for The Acrobrats? Do they sell them?' I try to make a joke, but actually that's what I think I need most of all, more than sneakers.

'Circus trainers!' she shrieks again. 'But you're a circus trainer. You can do that, Cedar. Why don't you?'

'No I can't, I don't know enough.' I shake my head but she has bent down to coo over Stinky and she's already distracted.

'We're off to the post-box,' I say.

She snorts and lets Stinky go, but as I walk off she yells out, 'But Cedar, you can do anything if you want to. So no excuses.'

I laugh and I wave at Pablo, who is sweeping the leaves off his driveway. I wonder why people bother sweeping up the leaves. Leaves always make the pavements much more colourful and much less official when they're lying around where they feel like lying. I don't say that to Pablo; instead I say, 'Hey, your garden's looking good.'

He frowns and scratches his head. 'Do you think so?'

'Yep.'

'It needs a good weed, really.'

'No it doesn't. All gardens need a few weeds in them just

to remind you of all the weeds you've got growing out of your own head. That way you know it's natural to be a bit out of control.'

Pablo laughs and I notice that I'm feeling better already. Sometimes you just need to get some air into your head, and then mix that with some nice neighbourly banter, and you lighten up. Easy!

picture of
section of
pavement
without leaves

and with .
leaves.

Stinky and I head up towards the shops so we can post Kite's letter, and I'm even beginning to feel a bit sprightly, as if I might just have to do a cartwheel. But I hold back, since I'm wearing a skirt and I don't want to flash my undies, which is lucky because as I round the corner I practically bump into Harold Barton. Imagine if he'd seen that. To tell you the truth, he isn't looking happy. He isn't even really looking. He's obviously thinking hard about something because he nearly bumps into me.

'Hey,' I say, 'watch where you're going.' He looks up and stops dead still, staring at me as though I'm an officer of the law and he's just murdered someone.

'Are you all right?' I say.

'Yeah,' he says, eyes still boggling.

'You don't look it.'

'Hey, Cedar, did you ever know your dad?'

'No, not really. You know he died when I was a baby. Why?'

He blushes and looks away and wipes at his mouth with the back of his hand.

'Nothing,' he says. 'Just wondering.'

We both stand there. It's awkward and heavy but there's something different. It's not a fight. It's not him against me. It's weird. I'm not used to it. I'm not even sure I can handle it.

'Oh well, see ya.' I start squirming off.

'Bye,' he says, and he drags himself off without even saying one smart-arse thing.

I shake my head in wonder. You never know, I say to myself, and I feel that it's the profoundest thought I've had all day. Because just when you think you *do* know someone, or you've got something all figured out, life makes sure you have to un-know it a little bit. Otherwise we'd all be big know-alls, and no one would ask questions anymore or leave gaps in their mind for new stuff. I certainly had a few gaping gaps in my mind that day, because after the entirely weird Harold Barton experience, who should come walking up the street but Inisiya, the mysterious refugee.

Chapter 19

'Hello,' I say.

Inisiya stops and looks at me with a questioning frown. Obviously I'm not as memorable as she is, or maybe she just isn't such a sleuth. She has a cool old canvas bag hanging from one shoulder and her eyes are shaped like almonds.

'I'm Cedar. I met you last week at the Fitzroy Learning Network. And I saw you once before in the street at night. You went into the Abutulas.'

She nods and her expression becomes friendlier. But she doesn't speak, so I go on. 'I live in the same street as the Abutulas. How do you know them?'

'The Abutulas?' She shrugs. 'They help us. My family, when we first come to Melbourne. We have today been having lunch, but now I am going to buy chocolate because everybody wants chocolate.'

Her accent is odd, every word sounds Australian but the order and the rhythm of them is different. She has some kind of other sound in her voice, a more round and deliberate sound.

'They want chocolate? Maybe I'll come with you. I'm
going that way, for a stamp,' I say, even though its probably
obvious to her that I'm going in the opposite direction and
have already posted my letter. Was I being a shonky
detective? Would she guess I was on a mission of discovery?

'Okay,' she says, and you can tell she isn't one bit suspicious.

So, as we wander back up the street, I begin to gently
prod her with questions. First of all I ask her how she finds
Australia, because I can't even imagine what Afghanistan is
like. I think of pale yellow ground and palm trees and houses
made of stone.

She laughs. 'Oh, Afghanistan is a beautiful country. Very
beautiful.' As she says this you can tell she's picturing it in
her mind, and it's as if whatever she's seeing makes her sad
because she seems to hold the memory quietly, then bends
her head forward to shelter it.

'Why did you leave?' I know this is a big question, and
one you maybe shouldn't ask because it must be painful to
have to leave your country, but the question just popped out
before I could catch it and hold it back. She turns towards
me with a frown.

'You've heard about the Taliban?'

I nod. She shrugs and tilts her head. 'You know what they
do? They stone you to death for nothing; even if you read a
book that is not the Koran.' I hold myself back from prodding,
because it doesn't seem right to prod now. It feels too big.

After a moment she sighs and says, 'There is no life in

Afghanistan for a girl. I was not free to go outside. Girls are not allowed. You get stolen or you get raped. Sometimes I prayed, "Just make me a boy so I can go outside, at least, just not stay inside all the time." It is really hard there. I get here and I think, "How lucky they are – the women, the ladies – at least they get to have a life." In Afghanistan the women have to go to the rule of the husband; women do not have any choices. Men can do anything they want to – they can hit them, they can make them have this much children. Women are just nothing, they are just to work, clean, look after men.'

She has become quite fierce and intense, as if it's important that I understand. She shakes her head sadly. 'I feel sorry for my people. They grow up being spiteful.'

'Yeah,' I shake my head with her, 'that's bad.'

She smiles, but it isn't a cheerful smile, it's an accepting smile, like when someone gives you something you don't want for Christmas, like a pair of pink shorts; you smile because that's just the way life is. You have to act as if you're okay with your shorts, even if you're not.

I change the topic to what I hope might be a happier one because I don't feel I know enough to talk well about extreme situations, and I am ashamed of how little I know.

'How long have you been here in Australia?'

'Three years now. At first when we arrive we are in Baxter detention and then we live in Adelaide. But we do not like Adelaide, so now we come here.'

'What was it like, in the detention centre?'

'Oh, you know, compared to how we live before we are glad to be there, at least we are alive and we have showers and food. For us it is not as bad as it is now because we come earlier, before the Tampa, and they are not so crowded, and we stay one year instead of for many years, and we are not separated from each other.'

I wonder what it must have been like for her before, if it was worse than being in detention, but I don't want to ask her about something that might bring back bad memories so I just say that I'm glad she has made it here to Australia, even if it isn't as beautiful as her own country.

She looks at me as if she is really looking, for the first time, to see who I am or at least what sort of a person I am. I look at her right back in the eyes; I'm not afraid of being seen, because I mean it, I really do. She doesn't say anything for a while and neither do I, but just before we part she bursts out:

'You know here some people tell me I am a geek. But I think, "You have the opportunity to get education, why not use it – instead you waste it?" I see girls, they just talk and talk, they do nothing else. I talk too, but I do my work. Like in our country, girls are dying for some education. Here people just waste their time.'

'Yeah,' I say again, as if I've never wasted time myself. But she's on a roll anyway; she keeps going,

'I feel bad, you know, because you have got such a good country and you do not feel grateful. Here people are so fortunate. They get to have everything. I mean, what else do you want?'

I can't answer her because I know there is lots that I want, and suddenly it doesn't seem right to be wanting when I can go and play in my street whenever I choose. As we walk back to our street, I can't get her words, *what else do you want?* out of my head. I think of me wanting to be a circus star, wanting it even more than ever now that the possibility of joining a real circus is here. I even think of Marnie always wanting to look pretty and great, and Mum wanting to one day buy a house, and Barnaby wanting to play his songs to the world. And then I think of all the girls in Afghanistan who just want to be able to go outside and play. It confuses me. Maybe wanting something is just what you do. It's not really about what you have or what you need, it's about something else.

And then I figure that there's all these people wanting all over the world, all wanting something, all wanting with all their hearts, all wanting just one bit more than what they already have. How do you know when what you have is enough? And if it is enough, why do you still want more?

Don't worry, I didn't hit Inisiya with any Philosophy According to Cedar B. Hartley. I just listened to her, and when I got home I asked Aunt Squeezy what she thought. She said there're two ways to make people richer: one is to give them more money and the other is to teach them how to desire less.

I went around for the rest of the evening practising believing I had everything I wanted, and it felt so very peaceful inside me I could hardly recognise myself.

Chapter 20

Not for long, though. I was woken up by the old familiar whirls of thinking and wanting. For one thing, I was thinking about Inisiya and how even though she was from a different land and spoke a different language and all that stuff she was still a girl, just like me or any other girl around. Just like a tree is a tree. In fact, if Inisiya was a tree she'd be a claret ash tree, because she seems to glow just the way a claret ash does in autumn. It's as if we all have trunks and leaves, but then we grow in different shapes and colours. Some people put more energy into their leaves, or stretch their branches in every direction; others concentrate on their trunks, and others become beautiful colours or bear fruits or blossoms or canopies of shade. Like I could never, even if I really tried, be a tidy tree or a tree that is part of a hedge, because I would have unruly bits sticking out. And then you get trees who just don't get enough sun, like hungry people or the people in Afghanistan who can't go out and play, so they have to reach more and then once they find the sun you have to hope it's not too late for them to lean into it and grow the parts that couldn't grow before. Because maybe they are good at reaching, like Inisiya. Not like Harold Barton, who has never had to reach for anything because his parents buy him anything he wants.

'Harold may have things, but he might not have people who understand him or show him love,' said Aunt Squeezy when I triumphantly filled her in on my new slant on trees.

I snorted unsympathetically and poured the cornflakes into my bowl. 'Anyway, I'm going to try and bump into Inisiya again because I've got things I want to give her, or if she doesn't need them she might know other refugees who do.'

Mum glanced up from the newspaper and smiled at me. I stuck my tongue out and said, 'It will keep my room tidier if there's less stuff in it,' because I didn't want anyone thinking I was trying to do a good deed. Good deeds are something Girl Guides do, and I don't like the way they smell.

For the next week I kept trying to bump into Inisiya, but it didn't happen. You never bump into anyone unless you're not expecting to. That's the nature of bumping. In the end, Aunt Squeezy suggested that she could invite Inisiya over for lunch when she saw her at the Network. I said that would be too formal and kind of daggy, but Aunt Squeezy said that Inisiya came from a culture that was very hospitable, anyway, and also she might not have ideas about what is and isn't daggy. So in order to prove that I, too, wasn't so superficial as to care about being daggy or not, I let myself be convinced.

Inisiya came for lunch the next Saturday. I really wanted to invite Caramella as well, but since I hadn't heard from her I figured she was still annoyed at me. And I couldn't handle two delicate situations at once.

When a good buddy like Caramella comes over you don't exactly want the grown-ups hanging around, but since I hardly knew Inisiya and I'd never before invited someone for lunch I was actually relieved that Aunt Squeezy and Mum were there to do all that nice welcoming, breaking-the-ice stuff, because that's one of the things grown-ups are better at. I only had to hover like a teenager and smile and make interested comments. Mum had made her famous vegetarian lasagne, and we all sat around the kitchen table and of course Aunt Squeezy drove the conversation because she knew what to say and she knew a lot of people that Inisiya knew. After lunch was over, she said to Inisiya, 'Cedar has got a pile of things together for you to take to the Network to see if they can be distributed to the others.' She looked at me. 'Why don't you show Inisiya your room?'

Aunt Squeezy should have been a diplomat.

It was a great way to get out of grown-up territory and into the land where kids grow. Bedrooms.

Once there, I flopped on my bed and let out a big breath to get rid of all the politeness.

Inisiya didn't seem bothered by it. She looked out the window and said, 'You got a lovely house.'

'It's not ours, really. We just rent it,' I said.

'In Afghanistan we have no windows in our house. The glass all got broke by the bombs and guns going off. So we have black plastic over them.'

'That must have been terrible. That means you couldn't even see outside.'

She shrugged. 'There are courtyards. You can go in them. We live all together, my grandmother and cousins.'

'Did they all come here too?'

'No.' She shook her head and stared out the window again, and I could tell she didn't want to talk about them, so instead I asked what she brought with her when she came because I was wondering what I would take with me if I had to leave my house and my street for ever. Stinky, of course; the photo of my dad smiling, my diary, my corduroy coat, my letter from Kite…But how would I say goodbye to Caramella?

'Nothing,' she said. 'Whatever luggage we take with us we have to throw it in the sea when we are on the boat.'

I tried to imagine throwing all those things overboard – the photo of my dad smiling, Stinky, my corduroy coat – but I couldn't. I couldn't imagine having nothing; nothing to guard your memories with, nothing to say 'this is me'. It made me panic, made me feel as if I would lose some of myself.

'Oh my God. Nothing! So what was it like to arrive here, like that, with nothing?'

She laughed and shook her head.

'No. We are so happy to arrive, finally. We no longer care about our things. We are happy to be alive.'

'Yeah, I guess…'

I looked at the pile of things I had made and wondered if any of it would be useful. Maybe things are only important when they mean something, and even then?

She looked at it too and smiled. 'It is nice of you to do that,' she said.

I felt silly, though, as if the things weren't nearly enough to make even a small difference. I drew our attention away from them.

'Well, what was it like to go to school? Could you speak English?'

'I learn as much as I can in detention centre. I talk to the securities, to practise. But still, Aussie kids talk different to how we learn English. At first, I cannot understand. Also, I am different from other kids.'

I looked at her and she didn't look different, she looked exactly like a teenager should look. She was wearing a black hippy shirt with embroidery on the front and hipster jeans and she had enviable golden skin that would never burn in the sun and turn to freckles like mine did.

'How were you different?' I said.

'Oh, you know, the clothes. Also they look and act different – even the teachers. And then, also, I do not know how to play. You know, I never play before in Afghanistan. I do not know monkey bars or netball or anything. At first

I hate school but my mother says to me, "You will speak one day English, and then you will like it.'"

I can't imagine how you could be a kid and not play. Isn't that what being a kid is all about? What kind of kids are they creating in Afghanistan? I wondered to myself, but I didn't say that. I said a really good thing. I said, 'Hey, have you ever been hedge walking?'

She giggled and shook her head.

'Come on then. I'll show you.'

One thing I know is there's nothing like a bit of playing to soften the edges of a new friendship. So that's what we did. We didn't talk about Afghanistan or black windows or lost cousins and things thrown overboard, we just went and climbed the hedge and hung there like two different-coloured parrots squawking on about girl things, like best friends and falling in love. I even told her about Kite.

Chapter 21

The next day I was in my room sorting through my things, determined to make more piles of stuff to give to the Learning Network for all those refugee kids who arrived here without anything. Don't worry, I wasn't becoming a Good Samaritan, it's just that I couldn't stop thinking about them having nothing. Barnaby popped his head into my room.

'God, what a mess! Phone call for you.'

I dragged myself away from my piles of things, vaguely hoping it might be Caramella, because I still hadn't heard from her since I slipped that letter under her door.

'Hello,' I say.

'Hi, it's Kite.' (*Voice slow and trickling.*)

'Kite! Wow. How are you?' (*I'm suddenly breathless.*)

'I'm good. (*Laugh.*) Hey, I just got your letter.'

'Did you?' (*What a stupid thing to say; he just said he did.*)

'Yeah. And I figured by the time I got round to writing back it would be too late, so I've rung you up instead.'

'That's good.'

'You still sound like you.'

'So do you.' (*Luckily.*)

'Anyway, I wanted to tell you that I'm really stoked you're going to come up.'

'Yeah?'

'Yeah. I reckon you've got a good chance of getting in. Only you have to work out a bit of an act, you know. Just the kind of stuff we were doing.'

'Oh.' (*How would I do that on my own?*)

'But also I was thinking you could help me with mine, because I want to do some of our old moves. There's a girl here, Lola. I've been practising with her and she's pretty good. She really wants to do it, so I have to let her know. But if you come, I'll do it with you.' (*There's a pause.*) 'You're lighter.'

'I bet she's better, though.'

'Nah, she probably knows more moves and she's got a really hot hoop act, but for this stuff you're just as good.'

'Oh.' (*Is she really pretty though, like Marnie?*)

'Anyway, I think it would help you get in if they see you do adagio, 'cause you're great at it.'

'Adagio? What's that?'

'Double balancing – that's what they call it here.' (*We never called it that.*)

'I see. Well, I'll try. I'm not sure yet how I'll get there…' (*What am I saying? I'm not even allowed to go.*)

'Aren't you going to come with Barnaby?'

'Barnaby? Is he going?'

'Yeah. He and I were talking about it before I left. He's doing a gig here at the Termo. I told him to bring you with him. That's how I knew you'd be able to make it, 'cause the audition just happens to be in the same week.' He laughs. 'Must be meant to be.'

'Yeah, right.' (*Pause, while I let all this sink in.*) 'Barnaby hasn't mentioned it to me yet.' (*Maybe Ada doesn't want me to go. Maybe he made a pact with Mum.*)

'Well, just tell him, tell him you're coming.'

'Okay, I'll tell him.'

'Yeah, great. It'll be ace to see you.'

(*I laugh nervously. Kite pauses. Perhaps there's an awkward silence.*)

'Anyway, I'd better get off the phone,' he says.

'Yeah, it's long distance.'

'Yeah.'

'Thanks for ringing.'

'No worries.'

'Bye.'

'Bye, Cedar.'

I hang up. My heart is swelling up and down. Maybe I feel swoony. Maybe if I was in a movie, in a long white dress, I would faint right now, but instead I just swan back to my room and flop on my bed.

And then I remember: Lola. It jerks me out of my swoon

in quite a disagreeable way. Lola who wants to be his adagio partner. Lola with the hot hoop act. If I don't go, Lola will be his new partner and then one thing will lead to another, like it did with us, and soon she'll be his new girlfriend (if she isn't already).

I absolutely have to go.

And then I remember: I'm not allowed to go. It completely sinks me into despair. I won't be able to live in Albury, I can't join the Flying Fruit Flies. I'm only pretending to myself that I can because I'm a mad, mad dreamer.

This is a dangerous thing to do.

Must stop it.

Must stop being a mad, mad dreamer.

I get up off my bed. I need to talk to someone, someone who isn't a mad, mad dreamer; someone sensible like Caramella. But then I remember that she doesn't seem to want to talk to me. So I sit there, stuck halfway, with my legs dangling and droopy. Can't dream, but can't get sensible either. I look at Stinky curled up in a hairy pile; he doesn't have to do either. Best thing to do when you're in a pickle, particularly a hotted-up one, is take some time out and pat Stinky. He always makes you relax a little, and when you relax you get more ideas. So I get down on the floor and Stinky starts thumping his tail in anticipation and I rub his ears, and just then Aunt Squeezy pokes her head in the door.

'Me and your mum are going down to the Learning

Network. They're having a party to celebrate the opening of their new back room. Want to come? It'll only be for an hour, and there'll be pizza, and you can bring that stuff you want to donate.'

Not really, I think.

'I guess so,' I say. After all, if you're looking for an idea, and someone just makes an offer, there's a good chance it might lead you somewhere.

We pile into the car and head down to Fitzroy. Barnaby doesn't come because he's too old for community parties. So am I, but I've got a potential new friend, so that's different. I'm hoping she'll be there and we can stand in some dusty corner and munch on pizza, and I'll tell her all about my unusual life, though it's going to sound just a little bit undramatic compared to hers. But still, a life's a life, drama or not.

When we get there, Aunt Squeezy goes directly to the bathroom because she has bad morning sickness and every now and then she has to spew. So Mum and I are left hovering in the hallway until Maude, who's wearing a red paper crown, ushers us into the computer club room, which has been transformed into a spread of large coloured cushions with seated Muslim ladies, who are wearing colourless robes and scarves and fussing over children.

Maude says, 'This is the women's room, but the food will be served in our new hall. Come and see.'

I scan the room for Inisiya, but she isn't there.

Out the back is a courtyard with a big old tree in the corner, an overhanging verandah and an old shed. There's a barbecue and trestle tables with plates of cake and dips and spring rolls and falafels and spinach cheesy things – but no pizza (never mind). Behind one table stands an old woman with a gumnut bob and a large nametag saying 'Elspeth'. She's serving drinks. Mum gets a wine and I get a lemon fizzy thing. The courtyard is full of people. Some are volunteers, others are refugees, and many of them are children. I watch a couple with a baby. The woman wears a lavender-coloured headscarf. She leans close to her husband and lowers her eyes, as if she's too shy to look at anyone. Clumps of men stand with hands in pockets. A very small Asian woman walks around with a platter of spring rolls, explaining, 'I make them dis morning.' She smiles at everyone, even me, as if she really likes me, which makes me instantly like her. I grab some cheesecake, because who can resist, and follow Mum to peek in at the hall. A small girl on a bright yellow plastic tractor pushes her way through the legs. There are children everywhere, wandering, playing, tugging, weaving an invisible thread through the adults.

I think how adults can't take off their shoes and play chasey, so they don't get to loosen their thoughts and their recipes for how to behave. They just stand still in one place, and the air around doesn't move them or bend them. Not like kids. Kids are kids before they're anything else; before they're Muslims, or Eskimos, or future Kings of England.

Because their beliefs haven't set hard yet, and they can still play, still be caught in a whoosh or a bang. If playing was a language, all the kids all over the world would be able to talk to each other, even if they were from the Mongolian desert, or the Bronx, or some toffy boarding school. Then I thought: once I'm Prime Minister there may not be wars, because no one will have to be so serious and dead-set about their beliefs, not if they can play.

I gallop on with this thinking because, boy, the ideas are flowing, and of course then I have the very best and most useful thought of the whole day. Here it is: since I'm not quite Prime Minister and I haven't got a country to fix, what if I could use the back room to teach circus skills to all the refugee kids, and Caramella and Oscar could come and help, and slowly we'd build up a new crew of Acrobrats? And, in the meantime, all the kids could learn something that would make them happy, just like it made me happy. And all the adults would come and watch and they'd see how good it is to play together.

I literally bounce out of the hall, just as if I've grown angel legs, to look for Aunt Squeezy and tell her my new great thought, leaving poor Mum in there to serve apple juice and act like an adult. I find Inisiya instead. She's sitting on a bench in the courtyard under the tree with another girl. They are both wearing the same school uniform: blue daks, sneakers and V-necked jumpers. But since I'm feeling all lion-hearted and brave, I just lumber over and say, 'Hi.'

Inisiya jumps up and beams and hugs me, just as if I'm an old friend. Then she turns to her friend and says, 'Remember I tell you about Cedar, who comes down here to volunteer? This is her!' She turns back to me. 'This is my best friend, Nidal.'

Nidal leaps up with a grin and hugs me too. I'm not sure if it was the roar of my newly forged lion-heart that makes them hug me, or if they just have a hugging custom, but it makes me feel so happy in a startled way that I almost forget who I usually am. Am I really so infected by the rules of cool that it could throw me, even in an upward direction, when someone is instantly warm? I shudder at the thought and quickly let myself soak up the warmth so that it will stay with me, like a suntan. I tell them my idea. Inisiya has her arm around Nidal, and leans into her every now and then.

When I've finished, Nidal says, 'It is a great idea.'

'I am double jointed,' Inisiya says, and she holds up her hand and bends her thumb back to touch her wrist.

'You can be the contortionist,' I say.

'Your aunt, she already ask me if I am interested in learning circus.'

'Did she really?'

'Yes, before she introduce us.'

'What did you say?'

'I say I think it would be great. Did she not tell you?'

'Nope, she didn't.'

I have to admit I felt a bit flattened. I felt like, all along, Aunt Squeezy was really the one with the idea and somehow she'd been gently nudging me towards it. But still…I shrugged. Who cares about that? I was the one who could pull it all together. That's something. It's all very well to have ideas, that's just like starting the engine, but someone's got to drive the car, know when to change the gears, turn a corner and how to fix a leak, and that's the hard part.

When we get home, I start to fix the leak. I ring Caramella.

'Guess what,' I say, and then I just go ahead and say it, because we all know Caramella never guesses anyway. 'The Acrobrats are back on the road.'

'Really?' she says, and by the sweet, rising sound of her voice, I know I'm forgiven.

Chapter 22

Of course, it wasn't that easy. There was a lot to organise before we could even start, and I'm not a good organiser. Neither is Oscar. Caramella is okay, but she's shy and slow. Luckily Aunt Squeezy was on board, because if there's too much boring stuff to do I can get feeble-witted, and drift. I'm a dreamer, not a manager, but as I said it's no good having ideas unless you can make them into real things, so I tried. I tried to act like a driver.

picture of common positions for mad mad dreamers to take up at school

First of all, Aunt Squeezy had to arrange a time when we could all come and when the back room was available. Then we had to find mats. In the end, Mum rang Ruben and asked about the ones we used to use in the garage. He said we were welcome to them, and that they were in storage in someone else's garage. So, eventually, we had mats. I had a meeting in our kitchen with Caramella and Oscar in which we talked about the best way to run a class, and what we could teach. Aunt Squeezy agreed to oversee the classes, since there had to be at least one adult supervisor.

As well as all this, I was making other plans, so I was busy. Suddenly I was lying awake at night trying to work it out. Here's what I came up with:

First of all, I get The Acrobrats up and running. In the meantime, I start working out my own act – for the audition. I've got about six weeks. In the other meantime, I return to sleuth mode, find out when Barnaby is leaving for the tour, and then stow away in the back of the car and catch a ride to Albury. Once I'm there I can stay with Kite and Ruben. (Will leave a note for Mum, of course.)

I do the audition, simply stun them all, they immediately offer me a place, Kite wraps me in his glorious arms and we go walk by the river, to celebrate.

Mum is so proud of me she agrees to let me stay with Kite and Ruben. But first of all I explain to the circus that I have a commitment back home with The Acrobrats and I will join the Flying Fruit Flies in four months time (which should be long enough to get The Acrobrats functioning without me); and because they want me so much, they let me go, but for four months only...

What is the meantime? Is it mean? Because it isn't real

time. It's a kind of secret, other time that goes on behind the
scenes while real time is performing its show.

I know, I know, there were a few weak links in the plan,
but I was sticking with it, anyway.

In the middle of all this, Ada comes for dinner. She
hardly ever does. Barnaby says she's allergic to family life.
I say we're hardly a typical family, so that's no excuse.

Ada comes in with Barnaby, wearing a strand of jade
beads high on her neck, a black singlet that is just slightly
see-through, and the same, distant, haunted expression she
always wears at our house. She folds her white arms across
her chest and stays close to Barnaby, although she smiles if
you smile at her, and when she smiles she doesn't seem as if
she's about to break out in hives. Barnaby sits her down and
gives her a beer. And then, just to make her feel not too
allergic, I say, 'I like your beads.'

Her hand floats up to her throat.

'Thanks,' she says, and she smiles again, but she doesn't
continue the conversation so I give up. I lean back in my
chair and say very loudly so everyone can hear, 'So, Barn,
what's happening with your tour plan?'

Mum interrupts and makes everyone sit down.

'Funny you should ask, Cedar,' says Barnaby. He sits down
as Mum plonks a chickpea curry on the table and yells for
Aunt Squeezy to come. 'We've had a change of plan,
actually.' He glances over at Ada, but her face gives nothing
away. My heart drops.

'We've been asked to do a festival in Sydney – Homebake, which is a great gig. They'll fly us up.'

'So you're not going to drive,' I say, while serving myself some rice and acting like it doesn't affect me one bit.

'Well, we'll fly Atticus up and then Adie and I might drive so that we can do a couple of regional acoustic shows on the way.'

Regional, I think. Does that mean Albury?

'Drive?' says Mum.

'Maybe,' says Barnaby.

'That would be nice,' says Aunt Squeezy. 'A little road trip, just the two of you.'

Ada blushes and sticks her fork in potato.

I say nothing. I feel as if my whole plan is teetering on a very fine edge.

'What car would you drive?' says Mum, suspiciously. She has her hawk eyes in and sniffer nose on.

'Well, Mum,' Barnaby pulls out his chair and smiles a nice slow smile, 'that's where you come into it.' (Barnaby doesn't have a car.)

Timing, I think to myself, what excellent timing. Barnaby always has that. Ask the big ask when someone else, someone not family, is around, so that Mum will feel obliged to be nice and agreeable. I'm proud of him. Mum sighs and rolls her eyes.

'How long were you expecting to take it for?'

'A week. It would just be easier than flying with the instruments. Also, we've got these gigs booked. But look, if it's a hassle Mum, we could cancel.' He leans forward with a concerned look. Another superb tactic. Make Mum feel responsible for them having to cancel a gig. Barnaby is an absolute master. I'm thoroughly impressed.

'No, no. Don't cancel. We'll see what we can arrange,' she mutters. You can tell she's a bit frustrated, but you can also tell that she'll let him use the car.

'I'll have to check the insurance. Make sure you're covered.'

Ada glances up but doesn't move her head. Barnaby looks sidelong at her with a grin.

'Thanks, Mum. You're a good bloke.'

He opens his arms, leaning back, as if the world has just entered them. I keep quiet. I'm dying to ask when they're leaving, but I'm scared I'll give the game away. So I shove some curry in my mouth to stop me opening it.

Mum sighs again. 'So, which week is it?'

'First week in December.'

Perfect! Absolutely perfect. That gives me a month to prepare. I gulp down my food.

'This curry's great, Mum.' I burst onto the scene like a trumpet waiting for its moment. I'm exuberant.

'Yes, it's lovely,' says Ada, and then we all look at Aunt Squeezy, who's holding her belly and looking funny.

She grimaces and says, 'I think I'll have to eat the canned peaches instead.'

Oh God. It's not easy being pregnant.

Must remember never to get pregnant.

Chapter 23

'I have balloons,' says Oscar, 'all blue.' We're on our way to the first circus class. Aunt Squeezy is driving.

'What for?' says Caramella.

'A warm-up game.' Oscar grins and taps his knee wildly, but he doesn't explain further, not till we get there.

We arrive half an hour before the class is due to start, so we can set up the mats. Inisiya meets us there. Oscar holds out his unsteady hand to her and says, 'Hello. I know you've had a hazardous journey.'

She looks perplexed, but shakes his hand and says, 'Yes.'

Caramella is shy, as usual, and just manages a small 'hello', but as we all start unrolling mats we also unroll our awkwardness a little and I put on my Stevie Wonder CD, which always helps. And then I start talking.

'So,' I say, 'do you think anyone will show up?'

'Probably not Mohammed, but all the rest,' says Inisiya.

'Why not Mohammed? Is he a mountain?' says Oscar.

Caramella laughs and looks at Inisiya. 'Don't worry, he's always saying stuff like that, you'll get used to him.'

'Mohammed will not come because he is too serious. He is the only one in his family who speaks English, because he is the youngest. So he looks after them all. He has so much responsibility. He will only work. The family are afraid still.'

'Oh, he's grown up too early?' says Oscar.

I feel sad for Mohammed, though I don't even know him. He must be the serious boy I saw here when I first came. It makes me suspect that if you don't learn to play when you're young, maybe you never learn. Maybe you become dead-set about your beliefs.

Luckily, Oscar has started to dance. He always beams when he dances, and it's a very contagious beam. The way he dances is more like a thrash than a boogie, and I notice Inisiya grinning as she watches him. He begins to scatter the blue balloons on the floor as if he's sowing seeds. Then he suggests we blow them up. This is his game.

As people enter, we tie a balloon around their ankle. The idea is that we must all try to stamp and explode each other's balloon while trying not to get ours stamped on.

'But why are they all blue?' asks Caramella, holding one up to the light.

'Because blue is the sky's reward; it has the largest promise,' says Oscar as he performs a rather heavy pirouette, which makes him look like a Hills Hoist.

Whether it's the promise contained in blue, or not, it

works. They all come in together, about fifteen of them.
Inisiya introduces us. The family of Hmong girls clump
together; the older one, Mei, holding the hands of the
younger ones. They all have round, soft faces and seem as
timid as Caramella, only they're so small and gentle I'm afraid
they might snap like a twig if you pull at their arms. There
are some African boys (Inisiya says they're from Somalia and
Sudan); also Inisiya's little sister, Parisa, and Rashmi from
Pakistan, wearing glorious pink sneakers; and Jarrah and
Hussein and Mali and Layla and others whose names I can't
remember after the first round of introductions.

As soon as the class is set to begin, I feel like an impostor.
I feel as if I'm a beginner acrobat pretending to be a teacher,
which I guess is kind of true so it's no wonder I'm
panicking. At least I still have *The Tumblers' Manual* that
Ruben gave me. That's my one piece of legitimacy. What if
they ask me to do a round-off into a back somersault? And
then what will they think when they see Oscar and
Caramella – the two most unlikely looking acrobats ever to
say, 'I'm in a circus'. Will they think they've been had?

Of course it's the other way round. The worse we are at
it, the better they seem to feel. As soon as I try to
demonstrate a very simple balance with Oscar, like this:

picture of balance
that's supposed to be
easy

Oscar wobbles and makes such funny sounds that they all laugh, and Rashmi jumps up and down and claps. And when we try some rolling, the same thing happens. The first roll we demonstrate is called a sausage roll, at least I call it that, and it isn't easy but it's kind of stupid so you laugh when you don't make it. Caramella can sometimes do it, but only in one direction. Oscar, however, just seems to fall on his side in a lump and then, to add to the lump effect, he cycles his legs in the air so he looks like a tortoise who can't get up. This again sends them into outbursts of laughter and they all leap up to try. Hussein gets it almost straight away and astonishes himself.

So the hotchpotch accidental crew of Oscar, Caramella and me provides just the right mix of attitudes, abilities and inabilities. Oscar provides the light relief and keeps everything always potentially silly, Caramella shows how to be gentle but persistent, and I provide the excitement, just because I'm the eager-beaver jump-in-and-give-it-a-go type. So, though not one of us can do a back flip, or precisely *because* not one of us can do a back flip, we seem to pull it off. The younger ones love Oscar, and seeing him as a leader makes me realise that he's really a naturally good clown. The shyer girls, like Mali and Mei and her sisters, are drawn to Caramella's gentle way, and then the more adventurous of them, like Sali, Hussein, Inisiya and Nidal, have me to drive them.

∗   ∗   ∗

After they've all left, Inisiya comes up and sits with us.
She's warm and beaming.

'Hey, it is a great success, do you think?'

Oscar blows out a big breath and says, 'Magic, I say. It was
magic.'

Caramella nods. 'We all deserve an ice-cream.'

So the four of us walk up to Charmaines and treat
ourselves to ice-creams, and it seems that The Acrobrats are
really back on the road. It's a different road but it's still
going, and that's the main thing.

Chapter 24

I decide to walk with Inisiya back to the flats where she lives. I'm feeling all brave and big and bold, because giving a circus class is so much better than giving some old things that now I don't need to so feel useless in the face of all that she's been through. Maybe Inisiya feels it too, because suddenly, without me even trying, we're talking about her life in Afghanistan. It started because I asked her about her parents.

'You know, in Afghanistan my father work in the post office and my mother is a teacher before the Taliban. When the Taliban come to rule, they lose their jobs and my dad has to go out on the streets and sell sugar. Mum could not work at all.' She leans forward and kicks an ice-cream stick on the ground, then she twists round to face me, her eyes dark and large.

'They take my cousin and they torture him. After many weeks they leave him on our doorstep. He is almost dead. That is when my uncle tells us we must leave Afghanistan or we also will be killed.'

I close my eyes and I'm shaking my head as if a very sharp rock had just entered it. Something inside me shrinks in the face of it – of torture and danger and death – as if it's too distant, too disturbing for me to understand, but I am looking back at Inisiya in a huge and wild way because I'm shrinking and stretching all at once. I want to be big. I want to say the right thing. I want to make a difference even though I know I can't.

'I can't imagine how terrible that must have been. Were you scared?'

'Of course.' She jerks her chin up, and to me she looks proud and brave. 'I am really scared. We sell everything to pay a smuggler to get us out, and then we have to travel for a very long time, always moving at night and then locked in hotels in the day. Sometimes we do not even know what country we are in. It is exhausting, you know, always always moving. Never going outside in the day. My mum, she is crying a lot.' She paused and then shuddered. 'The worst is when we are on an island somewhere, and we could not sleep at all because of these bugs that bite us all the night. I cannot tell you how bad it is to be sore and itchy all over.'

I take a big breath in. 'How long did you travel like that?'

'Four months. Then we are in Indonesia and there is a small boat to take many families like ours to Australia. The boat has two engines. Half way there, the main engine stops and the captain of the boat says we will have to turn back because the boat cannot make it to Australia with only one small engine. But all the families on board say that since we

will be sent back to Afghanistan if we return to Indonesia, we
will all die or be killed anyway, so we take our chances to make
it to Australia. The captain has to go on with one engine,
moving for two hours then stopping to give the small engine
a rest. That is when we have to throw all our belongings in
the sea. But still the small engine also dies and then we are
left in the middle of the ocean, thinking that now for sure
we die. You know, people start to pray. It is awful.'

'Did you think you would die?'

'Yes, we all did. But maybe the prayers are answered
because then there is a helicopter and you should see how
happy we are. We wave and stand up and shout and the
helicopter has sent an Australian naval ship, which takes us
aboard. It is so great. They have a big crate of green apples.
We are so hungry, we are all so excited, we crowd round the
apples, eating, crying…And then I have my first shower for
many months. There was even shampoo and soap.'

When she described this, she was so alive and intense that
it seemed the relief was still inside her. It made me feel it
too and I suddenly wanted to cry.

'What happened then? Where did the ship take you?' I
said, trying to steady myself.

'Oh, after that, they put us in Baxter detention centre. We
are there for a year and then we are released into Adelaide.
No one helps us there, and we do not know anybody. So we
move here. Mr Abutula picks us up from the bus station and
we stay with him until we are allowed to move into the

Housing Commission flats in Collingwood. You know he is a good man, Mr Abutula. He is always helping new refugees from Afghanistan who arrive in Melbourne.'

'But where was your dad?' I say. 'When you arrived I only saw you and your brother and mother. Did he stay longer in Perth?'

She looks down and shakes her head. 'No.' Then she looks at me and all the excitement has vanished from her face. It's as if a window that was once open and bright has suddenly slammed shut. 'He is killed by the Taliban before we left.'

'Oh God, I'm so sorry.' I feel it hit me in the chest. It makes me close my eyes. 'My father died too,' I say, 'in a car accident.'

She looks at me and her eyes are sad and wide, and for a minute we both stop walking.

'I am sorry for you too,' she says.

My heart starts to wobble and then there are tears in my eyes, which I blink away. I can't tell if I'm sad for her or for me, but I feel as if the sore part inside me has opened up because I can join Inisiya there and she can join me, and even if it's only in a small way I feel we have leant our hearts together; made a sheltering place in which we can both be together for a minute.

In fact, looking back, I guess that moment was like the first firm stone laid in a house that friends build to shelter their friendship, because somehow it seemed there was a reason that we had met, and we could, after all, share something that was huge and hard and real.

Chapter 25

The classes just get better as we go along. Watching everyone practise, I work out why circus is the best thing to learn. For a start, it's not serious. Let's face it, you can hardly be too serious about rolling and bouncing, so you can get out of your seriousness and into your floppiness. You absolutely have to discover the part of yourself that's willing to try and fumble and learn a little at a time without any of it really mattering. Because it's not as if you're disarming a nuclear bomb. Secretly, I wonder if it matters to do things that don't matter. Especially for kids who've had to worry a lot, who've never felt safe; kids who've lost family and home and all their belongings, including best friends, dogs and the right to play; kids with thoughts that are heavier than a small person can carry. It's better to carry another kid on your shoulders than that kind of weight.

There's Sali from Sudan. He's got no parents. He lived in a refugee camp for two years. He's only ten, but he's fearless physically. From the start, he was hurling himself around.

Sometimes I was afraid he would hurt himself, but by the third class he could already do a dive roll. Aunt Squeezy says she's never seen him come to life like that. He laughs all the time. He's even showing off, asking me to hold the hoop higher.

Mohammed sometimes appears for a moment, stands in the doorway, but leaves as soon as anyone notices him. I've never even seen him smile.

After the class, I stay behind. I'm kind of exhausted but also determined. I have to make up a good act for the audition. And I have to practise my handstands, my round-offs. I have this idea that what I want to be able to do is a handstand on a
skateboard, like
this:

The problem is, the only person I can think of with a skateboard is Harold Barton, and as if he's going to lend it to me. As if.

I get on my bike and head home. I take the back streets, ride on the road and keep thinking. See, I haven't told anyone, not one single person, not even Caramella, about my plans and, let me tell you, it's killing me to keep such a big secret. It's unnatural for a girl like me. I'm getting pressure-cooked inside and I can't open the lid one little bit, even though I'm

about to steam up and burst. I can't tell Caramella or Oscar
because they'd think I was deserting. I can't tell Aunt Squeezy
because then she'd be torn between Mum and me, and I
obviously can't tell Barnaby because he's not on my side.
Besides, Mum would kill him if he took me up to Albury
without telling her, so I have no choice but to stow away.

Anyway, I quite like the idea of stowing away. It adds a
certain thrilling edge to the whole plan. Unfortunately, just
as I am basking in the glory of me as a stowaway, I notice
that I'm swerving, as I only have one hand to steer since the
other is caught in my jumper, which I am trying to take off
without stopping, and now I'm heading straight for a pole.

I have a suggestion to make to you.

Never try to take off a jumper while riding a bike and
dreaming up glorious situations all at the same time. Because
it's absolutely humiliating when you crash into a No
Standing pole with a jumper over your face and one elbow
thrust in the air.

Not only that, it hurts.

Not only that, other people could see it happen,
especially if it happens right opposite the tram stop on
Nicholson Street.

picture of a crash.

'Hey, Klutz, I thought you were s'posed to be
coordinated.'

It's Harold Barton. He's sauntered over from the tram
stop and he's laughing, though it actually seems he's trying
not to. I don't give him a second look. Instead, I'm picking
myself up and inspecting the damage. Blood and bruise on
the ankle, handlebars kind of twisted.

'Yeah, well I *am* coordinated. I can't help it if the pole
isn't. Didn't you see it swerve towards me?'

Harold actually bends down and picks up my backpack.
He ignores my excellent comeback and focuses on the bike.
'Boy, those handlebars are rooted.'

'Yeah.' I know nothing about handlebars but I forlornly
agree, only because I want to get Harold in an agreeable
mood. (I believe in signs, and this can be the only good
reason to have crashed so inelegantly.) It seems I am meant
to ask him. First I wind up my jeans so as to reveal my
bloodied ankle injury, then I limp forward in a pitiable
manner.

'Hey, Harold, maybe I could borrow your skateboard?'

'Why? So you can steer it into a pole?' His voice has
gone sneery again. Already I'm beginning to regret asking.
There's nothing he'd like more than to be able to withhold
something from me.

'No. I've got a job in Fitzroy. Every Wednesday. Now my
bike is stuffed, I thought I could use a skateboard for
transport. But, hey, there's plenty of other people I can ask.'

I turn around and decide to limp away, dragging whatever shred of dignity I have left with me.

I've gone at least five fragile steps before he yells out to me, 'Hey, Klutzo, if you tell me the truth, it's yours.'

I stop. Could I even contemplate really telling Harold Barton the truth? Of all people, he's the least trustworthy, the least deserving, least sympathetic, yet the most likely to be able to lend me a skateboard. Before I know it, I've spun around.

'Harold, can you keep a secret?'

He raises his eyebrows and gives an ever so slight nod.

That's all I need. After all, I just crashed, and maybe my lid fell off in the moment of impact. In fact, maybe I just need to tell someone, anyone. While I'm telling him his expression doesn't change, not even when I mention the stowaway bit. There's no sign he's impressed, nor even interested, though he doesn't seem uninterested, either. Of course, I leave out the most important truth, which is the fact that I'm in love with Kite and if I don't get up there I might lose him to Lola, the hot, hip-whirling hoop girl. Let's face it, Harold Barton wouldn't understand romantic plot points.

After I've finished, Harold frowns and starts to ask me questions about the Flying Fruit Fly Circus, which I answer impatiently since I don't actually know much; and also I want to get on with the deal, which was that if I told him the truth he'd let me use his skateboard for my act.

'Well, I'll think about it,' he says, pulling the peak of his cap down over his face.

'You'll think about it?'

'Yeah.'

'But you said if I told you the truth you'd hand it over.'

'Yeah, well I'm considering whether the truth is worth it, aren't I?'

I look at him contemptuously, and if he can't see me because his cap is pulled down so low he can surely feel the heat. I don't even answer. I'm too mad. I just turn my back on him with a loud sigh and start pushing my rooted old bike home, and slowly I begin to worry. Why oh why did I trust a big faker creep like Harold Barton? What if Harold Barton blows my plan? He only has to mention it to Mum and all will be ruined. The more I think about it, the bigger the worry becomes. And by the time I get home I'm an anxious, limping wreck.

Chapter 26

That evening, Aunt Squeezy comes home with an ultrasound picture of her baby. I'm sorry to say, but it looks like a large beetle. Mum sticks the photo on the fridge, but Aunt Squeezy seems sad. I tell her not to worry, probably even I looked like a beetle when I was a growing thing inside my mother and now look, I'm almost normal – well nothing like a beetle, anyway.

picture of me if I were
a beetle

Aunt Squeezy says that isn't what's making her sad, she's just sad that she's alone. I tell her she isn't alone because we're her family and I'll help her change nappies and so will Mum. Barnaby probably won't, but he'll do other stuff like put the baby on his shoulders just the way Dad is doing to me in the photo I have of him.

I know that Aunt Squeezy might prefer a real dad to carry her baby on his shoulders, so I say, 'You know what? I never really had a dad and look at me, I'm okay. A little unusual and a bit demanding and occasionally unruly, but still, if you get a good mum you can survive. Look at Inisiya, she doesn't have a dad either and she's not even unruly. Also, there's other possible dads you can find, like Ruben.'

Aunt Squeezy grins and glances briefly at Mum, who blushes and sinks into a chair, probably because I just said she was a good mum. But I can tell Aunt Squeezy has given up her sadness because she seems interested in my dadless theories.

'So, you like Ruben?' she says. Before I have a chance to answer, Barnaby himself walks in. He's holding a skateboard, which he puts on the floor, points in my direction and pushes towards me with his foot.

'Courtesy of Harold Barton,' he says, eyebrows raised. 'I thought you guys were enemies.' He gives Mum a look and she in turn gives me one.

'We are.' (I feel the panic rising again.)

'Well, he was just leaving this on the doorstep when I arrived, and he asked me to give you this as well.' Barnaby reaches into his back pocket and with another suggestive grin he flicks an envelope across the table. It's sealed and it has my name written on it.

Just to prove there's nothing schmaltzy going on between Harold Barton and me, I grab the letter and rip it open in front of everybody. Inside there's another sealed envelope addressed to the Flying Fruit Fly Circus, plus a note that says, 'Good luck with your trip to Albury. Please pass this letter on from me to the head of the Flying Fruit Fly Circus. Thanks, Harold.'

Boy, am I in a pickle. I can't read that aloud. I feel the blood creeping up towards my face and I desperately dive into my mind to find a way out. It delivers me with a brilliant half-truth.

'Oh, it's just, he wants me to forward a letter to Kite. That's all. The skateboard's a bribe, I guess.'

'A bribe,' says Mum. 'You don't even use skateboards.'

Luckily, Barnaby steps in before I have to deal with that one.

'Hey, why don't you give it to me, then? I can deliver it next week when I pass through Albury.'

I'm not sure if he believes me. I can't tell if he's testing me, laying a trap, or if he's just trying to be helpful. (Unusual.)

'Nuh,' I say, standing up. 'It's okay. I'll send it, 'cause I've got to send one of my own anyway.' I look away from Barnaby because he knows me well enough to see through any faking, and then, just because I'm feeling a bit hot under the collar, I pick up the board, tuck it under my arm and slink out saying, 'Anyway, I'm going to see if it's any good.'

'Don't be long, dinner will be ready soon,' calls Mum, as I bang the door behind me.

It's unusually quiet in the street. Our street is a dead end, a small dead end, so there's no through traffic, which makes it seem like it's just ours, as if all of us who live here own the street. Which is why people like Ricci and me and Caramella and the Abutulas treat the street like it's our front garden – for hanging out in. But this afternoon I'm the only one here. I sit on the board.

For one thing, I'm burning, burning, burning to open Harold Barton's letter to the Flying Fruit Flies. Even though he's given me the skateboard, it all seems a bit suspicious, a bit Secret Operation. It isn't ticking or anything obvious, but I stare at the envelope. Why did he just leave it at the door? I still don't trust him. I still figure he must be up to something. But does that entitle me to open a letter that's not addressed to me? I have a feeling it doesn't. This is an annoying feeling to have. It's getting in my way, creating a little battle in my head between what I want to do and what I know I shouldn't do. I stuff the letter in my back pocket and try a handstand on the skateboard, which is much harder than I thought it would be. Luckily, the challenge it presents takes over and for the next half hour I doggedly try and try to hit a balance, and I forget about the letter (at least until a week later when I am packing my bag for my stowaway trip to Albury).

After about fifty tries, I heave a big huff and march over

to Caramella's. She's on the couch, cross-legged, doing a drawing.

'Hey, Caramella, can you help me? I need some spotting. I'm trying to do a handstand on a skateboard but I can't seem to hit it.'

'Why are you trying that?' she says.

'What are you drawing?' I go over and have a peek. It's a pencil drawing of a sad, young face. I don't know how she makes it look sad and young, because the mouth isn't turned down. The sadness is in the eyes. Caramella screws up her face at the drawing, and holds it away from her.

'The drawing's wrong,' she says.

'It's very sad,' I say. 'I think it's a great drawing.'

'It's meant to be Mohammed,' she says. 'Not exactly him, but you know, something of him.'

Mohammed is the Afghan boy who never joins in; the one who just appears in the doorway like a small, dark ghost. I realise that it isn't exactly sadness that's in the face, but an absence, a sense that something isn't there.

'It looks as if he's haunted,' I say, and I wonder if he remembers what he has lost.

'Yeah. He is. I wish he could join in but I think he's shy. I think he's proud too. He's afraid he might make a fool of himself.'

I look at Caramella with her soft, round face studying her drawing, and I can see she has really been thinking about Mohammed, and she's concerned. I think even in some way she might feel she understands him. I remember how shy she was when I first dragged her along to training, how she glued herself to the wall pulling her T-shirt down and how, bit by bit, she became more willing to have a try.

'After all,' she says, looking up at me as she stretches her legs and puts the drawing down, 'that's the point, isn't it? I mean, the whole reason we're teaching circus there is to teach them something that makes them enjoy themselves.'

'Yeah. For sure. That's the point. But also it's good for anyone to feel they're learning something. You keep trying and you get better at it. That's why I just tried to hit a balance on a skateboard.'

'And still you haven't given up?'

'No way.'

Caramella laughs.

'Ah, Cedar, that's when you're great. That's when you're at your best. When you don't give up.'

We both look at each other. I'm sitting on the back of the couch. There's a tiny serious moment when I have a feeling that she's just said something meaningful, something that reaches further than skateboard hand balances. I know it has something to do with me giving up on the circus, and then not giving up on the circus. Sometimes your own importance wells up way beyond your self and submerges the real things, the things that count. I guess meeting Inisiya had reminded me that the circus didn't have to be about me, it could be about something else, about the things Caramella was talking about. I feel very warm right then, in that serious moment, and without really knowing exactly why I reach down and give Caramella a big hug. And then I drag her outside to spot me while I keep trying to hit that balance. I'm like a dog with a bone when I really want to learn a new trick.

Chapter 27

So, it's the night before my great adventure and I'm secretly packing my things. I'm trying to take as little as possible, since I need to be slim and streamlined enough to slither into the back of a Holden without looking like a small, quivering human bump.

Let me tell you, it's very hard for me to take only a few things as I tend to imagine situations in which I might need a tennis racquet or a candle or a pineapple, or Barnaby's lava lamp, or even a very glamorous dress…Just imagine I'm living with Kite and Ruben and one night a visitor from Argentina arrives and decides to teach us all how to tango. Well, a long dress would be essential and a lava lamp would very much add to the atmosphere.

But since I don't have that kind of a dress or a tennis racquet, and Barnaby would kill me if I took his lava lamp, which is lilac, I managed to cut it all down to two green apples, trackie pants and singlet, torch, bathers, nightie, a book called *The Road Less Travelled*, which Aunt Squeezy lent me, my diary, the skateboard and of course Harold Barton's letter (still burning, burning, burning).

When I go to bed the night before Albury, it feels a lot like the way the night before Christmas used to feel when I was little. I'm so excited it takes me a long, long bout of thinking and dreaming before I fall off to sleep. And by the time I get up the next morning, I'm beginning to have fears instead.

What if Barnaby and Ada discover me early and kick me out of the car?

How will I cope with the disappointment, the humiliation?

What if I make an absolute fool of myself at the audition?

What if I really do get into the circus and I have to move to Albury without Mum?

And what if Stinky can't come and live with me?

I start to feel very lonely. I wish someone was going with me. I wish even Caramella could pop over and say, 'goodbye, good luck.' If only I could take Stinky, the little hairy guy, with me. I try to distract myself from these thoughts by rolling out of bed just as if it was a normal day. But as soon as Stinky hears I'm up he noses his way into my room for a pat, and I pull him onto my lap.

Sometimes I think I love Stinky too much. I mean it makes me scared how much I love that dog. Once you love someone, even a dog someone, even a cockatoo, you start thinking that life would be unbearable without them. Maybe not everyone thinks that, but I do, because I can't stop my imagination running away, running like an untamed horse, windswept and blustery, through the forests, sometimes going to wildly sad places and sometimes to wildly great places, but there's no doubt it's got the taste for roaming and if it comes across an idea that maybe one day Stinky might not be here it can be so utterly convincing that I start feeling unbearably sad. And I mean unbearably. But then there's not much you can do because you can't subtract your love to make it less. You can't close it up or tie it down. Once it's out, it's out, and you can't get it back in. Imagine if everyone could measure out the exact amount of love they were willing to gamble. But even if I could do that I reckon I'd still be a gambling man, I mean a high roller, like my Aunt Squeezy. She's always giving too much love, especially to Italian cads. Can you do love too much? I know there's a lot of things that you shouldn't do too much, like telling lies, watching telly (especially up close – it makes your eyes square), showing off, eating green apples off Caramella's tree (gives you the runs), but I never heard anyone say, 'Now now, don't you go and love that person or that dog or you'll get the runs.'

Oh, life is very, very big.

*   *   *

I go eat breakfast and I act as normal as possible. Mum, as usual, is racing out the door with a piece of toast in one hand, keys in the other. She kisses me goodbye, says, 'Hey, vegie lasagne for dinner tonight,' because she knows it's my favourite.

I say, 'Mmmm-mmm, great,' just as if I'm really excited about that.

A minute after she has left, she comes back, bursting in with a frown and unwinding a car key from her keys and whacking it on the kitchen table.

'Cedie, tell Barn when he gets up that this is the only car key I've got so he can't lose it. And also could you remind him to check the oil and water and pump up the tyres and, oh God, he's so vague – he's likely to blow the head gasket.'

'Mum, you'll blow your own head gasket if you don't stop worrying,' I say.

She grins again and rushes out with a wave, leaving me alone with the smell of toast and a small, sweet, fond feeling for her. She's a good mum, I think to myself, just as all soldiers think when they lean out the train window and wave goodbye to their weeping mothers on the platform. I don't dwell on this for too long; instead, I begin to make myself scrambled eggs on toast, not my usual breakfast but one that most brave journeymen must eat before a big day. As I scramble the eggs I go over the plan:

1. Make like I'm going off to school, just as always (have already sussed out estimated time of departure is midday).

2. Instead, go down to creek and practise pole positions and audition routines.
3. At about eleven-thirty, sneak back and wedge myself and my pack on car floor behind front car seats, cover with picnic rug.
4. Lie very still and begin to pray.
5. After car has left, wait at least one and a half hours so that it's too far out of town to be sent back, then reveal myself directly. Make a very good joke so that Barnaby will not be too mad.

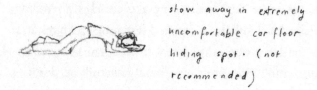

slow away in extremely uncomfortable car floor hiding spot. (not recommended)

But it is somewhere between step three and four that the story doesn't quite go according to plan. This is what happens: I've managed to wriggle down and cover myself up. Luckily, the back seat has already been pushed down and this almost covers me. Barnaby and Ada are packing the car, shoving guitars and amps in the back. Aunt Squeezy is helping them. I'm hardly breathing. The car door near my head opens and someone is pushing things around. Aunt Squeezy is saying, 'Have you got water? What about taking some fruit?' And then suddenly the blanket is ripped off my head and I'm staring at Ada and she's staring at me. She's frozen, half bent down with a pillow under her arm, and so am I, eyes cranked up towards her imploringly.

Barnaby is calling from the boot, 'Hey, Ada, did you put the doona in?'

She doesn't answer him. She opens her eyes wider as if to make sure she really is seeing what she thinks she's seeing, and I put my finger to my mouth.

'Adie?' says Barnaby.

I feel my face contort in alarm, which she must register as well, because suddenly she snaps out of our frozen exchange and she stands up.

'Yeah, I put it in,' she says. 'I'm just stuffing the pillows behind the seat.' She bends down again, looks at me in a slightly confused way, as if maybe I'm something she can't quite recognise. Then she quickly stuffs the pillow under my head and covers me up. A few minutes later, we're on the road.

I can hardly believe it. I can't believe Ada didn't blow my cover. I lie there picturing myself in years to come, telling the story while wearing something cavalier like a slanted felt hat. I'd be saying, 'I can't believe the dame didn't blow my cover. Man oh man, was I one lucky son of a bitch.' But, to tell you the truth, I don't actually dig that expression 'son of a bitch'. It's like making out that dogs and mothers are the ones to blame. So I wouldn't say it exactly that way.

I'm very uncomfortable, and doubting that I can keep still for the planned one and half hours. It's bumpier and smellier and stuffier than I ever imagined. Luckily, it's not long before Ada strikes up an intriguing conversation with Barnaby.

'Hasn't Cedar got a boyfriend at Albury?'

Barnaby laughs. 'Yeah, kind of. I don't know if it's got to that yet, but there's something going on. He's in some circus up there.'

Ada says, 'I guess she would have liked to have come with us then.'

Barnaby doesn't answer for a minute and I feel a squirm coming on. Then he sighs.

'Yeah, probably. Well, before Kite left he told me there'd be auditions towards the end of the year, because I told him that we might be passing through Albury on tour. He said not to tell Cedar straight away because he'd have to find out first whether she could audition. But if she could, we planned that I could bring her up.'

Ada says, 'So? What happened?' I'm really beginning to like Ada. Thank God for Ada.

Barnaby says, 'Well, turns out you have to live in Albury if you want to join that circus, and Mum can't possibly move there. Mum said she'd spoken to Cedar about it. There'd be no point in her doing the audition if she can't join.'

'Oh,' says Ada, and then there's quiet, just the sound of wind through the windows. I imagine that outside there are fields of yellowed grass with black cows lying down.

Then Ada says, 'Can't she live with some other family there, like a boarder?'

And I think, what a great idea. How come I didn't think of that?

Barnaby says, 'I don't know. I just think it would kill Mum, you know, if Cedar left home now. Mum's lost enough already. Anyway, Mum reckons Cedar wants to go more for the boy than the circus, and those kind of teenage crushes, they pass. She'll meet someone else and forget all about Kite and the circus.'

Forget all about Kite and the circus? Like hell I will. I can hardly stop myself from sitting bolt upright and putting him straight.

Luckily, Ada says, 'Do you think? I mean do *you* think so? She seems pretty determined to me. I reckon she seems to feel quite strongly.'

Barnaby says, 'Yeah, but that's Cedar. She just feels strongly about anything. She feels strongly about sultanas in the muesli. She's like me.'

I get a feeling there's a bit of a romantic moment going on now. I can tell by the tone in Barnaby's voice, which has gone tender-hearted. And there's almost the quiet, soundless sounds of blushing and touching and eyelashes, and I start feeling squeamish and like I'm about to suffocate in the stench of sentiment, until Ada sighs and starts fiddling around in the tape box for music. She puts on some mournful lady with a piano, and the conversation turns to music. After a while, they pull in for petrol.

I'm actually busting for a wee myself, and I'm really

straining my otherwise feeble ability to be still and quiet. So, while they are both out of the car, I push off the blanket, have a stretch, let out a few cheery sounds and peek out the window. The Billabong One Stop. A middle-of-nowhere truck stop. A weird skinny guy with dark glasses and a footy vest walks by, twisting an ice-cream wrapper. He doesn't see me but I see him. I also see that we're in the country now, so I happily hunker down again because I'm pleased I'll be able to reveal myself soon.

After we take off again, Barnaby changes the music and puts on 'G Love and Special Sauce'. One of my favourites. Then he says, 'Hey, Ada, I want to send Cedar a postcard. It's a list. Can you write something down for me? The title is: A List of Creek Names Between Melbourne and Albury. So far, Two Mile Creek, Faithful Creek, Turnip Creek, Black Dog Creek and Pelican Floodway.'

'Pelican Floodway? Is that a creek?'

'I don't know, but she'll like it.'

Pelican Floodway

A little while later, he says, 'You know, the thing about Cedar is that some of the time she fixes her heart so strongly on something she doesn't really see it for what it is. You know what I mean? She's going to think this circus in Albury is the be-all and end-all. And I just don't want her getting too disappointed if it doesn't turn out to be what she thinks it will be.'

Ada doesn't reply. But Barnaby seems to be in the mood for speech-making, anyway. What would he know? He's never even done a proper cartwheel in his life.

'I mean, I think the glamour of it is exciting for her. She's got this idea that it's a "real" circus, whereas the one she's in now with her friends isn't.'

The glamour of it? As if I give a stuff about that. Only I do like the idea of touring the world – who wouldn't?

Ada says, 'Still, she has to make her own decisions about what's best for her.' (Well said, Ada, you're a champ.)

Barnaby says, 'Exactly. In fact if I was her I would've just stowed away in the car and come along to see.'

Ada says, giggling, 'So you wouldn't have been mad with her if she had stowed away?'

Barnaby says, 'Nope. In fact, I just accidentally bought a double choc Magnum ice-cream, in case she had, but since she hasn't I may as well eat it myself.'

At this point I throw off the blanket and sit up with a big snort.

'Okay, okay, hand it over then, 'cause I'm starving.'

Without even looking, Barnaby passes it over his shoulder and says to Ada, 'So, looks like we've got ourselves a real live stowaway.'

Ada turns around and winks, and I mouth the word 'thanks'.

'Looks like it,' I say, and I'm so relieved that Barnaby's not chucking me out that I settle back and start singing along to 'G Love' as loudly as I can. I watch the fields and the sky with the glorious, glowing feeling of my adventure really being under way.

Chapter 28

Before we get there, Barnaby says, 'So, little champ, where were you planning on staying?'

I hadn't actually planned beyond Step 5, of course. In some ways I hadn't dared believe I'd actually get beyond it. So I sit there with my mouth open like a big dumbo.

'Because at the Termo, where we're playing, they've got a room for us. We could probably smuggle you in there.'

I know where I want to stay and where I'd imagined I would stay, and it wasn't crammed in between Barnaby and Ada in some grungy hotel room.

'No, I'll stay at Kite's,' I say, 'only he isn't exactly expecting me. Well, he is, but he isn't expecting me exactly now. Actually, he doesn't know when to expect me because, see, I wasn't sure I'd, you know, make it or not.'

Truth was, Kite and I had never discussed accommodation, but I wasn't going to let on quite how disarrayed my plan actually was. At least I had the address and I was sure that if I just showed up they'd let me stay. That's what folk do in the country.

The problem is that when we do show up, there's no one home. The house is a nice big yellow wood house with a huge oak tree, just like ours.

'Look,' I say. 'Just leave me here and I'll wait. They can't be long.'

'We can't just leave you. Imagine. I'm going to have to call Mum and let her know you're with us. I'm not saying we just left you on a doorstep.'

After a lot of arguing, I persuade Barnaby to leave me on the doorstep. The plan is: if I don't call him in an hour to let him know I'm safe, he'll come back and get me.

'Give me two hours. It's light. I've got a good book. Look.' I flash *The Road Less Travelled* at them.

Barnaby says, 'You've got 'till 5.30.'

I want to be alone when I see Kite. I don't want big brother hanging around. I want to look like a brave traveller, a fearless risk-taker But also I want to look like I'm completely alone in the world so that he feels obliged to offer me lodgings. Let's say, brave – slightly ravaged from effect of long journey – orphan, in need of loving care, waiting on the doorstep, is the feel I'm going for. So it simply won't suit the story if Barnaby and Ada are with me. Not at all.

I'm relieved when they go, even though I've changed my opinion of Ada. In fact I have myself a little think about her. Aunt Squeezy says Buddhists try not to have opinions, because it can make you righteous, which means you always think you're right and you don't listen to other possibilities like, for instance, 'you're wrong'. But sometimes you don't realise you develop certain opinions until life does something to show you and your opinions up.

I had an opinion that Ada was kind of snotty and superior, but now I think she's just quiet around other people. Maybe she's even shy. Whatever she is, she's got an understanding heart because not only did she not blow my cover (not until the Billabong One Stop, anyway), I reckon she also tried to make Barnaby understand where I'm coming from.

So, I have a good think about opinions. I get a pile of stones and I put them on the front verandah, and then I get a bit of chalk and I draw a big head shape around the stones, like this:

The head represents my head, and the stones represent all the opinions I have in my head, making my head heavy and impenetrable. And then I try to work out what these opinions are, because once I know them I'm allowed to take the rocks out of my head and throw them away. The idea is to get my head to look like this:

"light and spacious"

The first opinion I pull out is this:

"Ada is upherself"

That one's easy because I've already kind of dislodged it. But I needed an encouraging take-off. The next one is harder:

"Harold Barton is a big phoney try-hard"

I put the stone on the borderline because I can't really be convinced I've let go of that opinion.

So then I try switching from people to other stuff like:

"if I dont become a circus star my life will be finished."

Strangely, it's just as I am catapulting that opinion out of my head that two brown, blistered feet in thongs enter the picture:

Before I have a chance to connect that thought to action, I hear Kite's voice. That low, running voice.

'Cedar?'

'Yeah?' I look up. I have a stone in my hand. He's grinning, not with his mouth but with his eyes. There's a large bag slung over his shoulder, which he's holding onto with both hands. He's wearing trackie daks and he looks messy and warm and entirely lovely. I feel like I'm going to do something stupid, something joyous and uncontrollable. In fact, even though it's only seconds, it seems like ages that we stay like this, with me crouched down and gazing up and taking in the look of him, like I'm taking in a big breath and it's making me dizzy.

He laughs, 'So you've arrived!'

'Yep.'

'I'm glad.'

At this point in the conversation I drop the rock and stand up and all I can think is, Should I kiss him hello, or will he kiss me? Because that's how I'd imagined it should be. A big kiss and then a long hug, just like when some guy comes home and surprises his girlfriend who's waiting and waiting, sighing on a swinging chair. Just like in the movies. But, of course, this is not how it happens. Maybe it's because he's holding that big bag over his shoulder and he has no spare arms to hug me with, but we both stand there, smiling; neither of us moves closer.

He looks down at my head drawing and he says, 'Rocks in your head?'

'Opinions, actually.'

He shrugs. 'Same thing I guess.'

'Yeah.' I laugh, and sweep all the rocks away with my foot then I look up at him, and I'm trying to look happy and confident, which isn't how I feel, so I don't know what comes out on my face – maybe there's a battle in my eyes – but whatever it is it makes him drop his bag and come towards me and, as if I am a homesick child, he hugs me and says, 'Hey, welcome to Albury, Cedar.'

'Thanks,' I mumble into his shoulder, and I breathe in the smell of him, which is all hot and sweaty and familiar, and for a minute I do feel all emotional but I have no idea why, so I quickly pull away and change the subject.

'Have you been training?'

'Yeah. I must stink.' He gets a key from his pocket. 'Let's go inside. Have you been waiting long?'

I shake my head as he opens the door and picks up his bag.

'Dad will be home soon. He'll be happy to see you. Where's your stuff?'

I pick up my tiny bag of 'stuff' and he laughs.

'You sure travel light.'

'Kind of, but see I've got a lot of rocks in my head to carry as well.'

He smiles, and I wonder if he knows what I mean. After all, we haven't ever really talked about stuff like that: opinions and compassion and Buddhists and bigots. As we go inside, I wonder if we could.

Chapter 29

Albury is bigger than I imagined. In the main part of town there are lots of grand old brick buildings with awnings, like proud eyebrows, to shade the streets. You can tell that it's an old town, which makes it kind of stately. There's modern stuff too: big shopping malls and takeaway joints, and young blokes screeching around in panel vans with flames and loud engines. This makes you think it's not quite so stately. So you think one thing and then you think another, which means it's complex and that's how a city should be. It's bigger than your average country town because the town centre isn't just one main road like I thought it would be, it's lots of main streets with all kinds of traffic on them, almost like a city. And then the houses are mainly nice old weatherboards with big gardens, like the yellow house where Kite and Ruben live. I even begin to think Albury wouldn't be a bad place to live, if only it weren't so far away.

At dinner that first night, Ruben talks a lot about Albury and the circus. He says how it had made a huge difference to a country town, where usually there is very little opportunity for the arts to flourish. But here, because of the Flying Fruit Fly Circus, every kid has a chance to be introduced to the arts, or at least to get an idea about how beautiful the arts can be. Also, the great thing about traditional circus is that it's for people who don't fit in; you can be any shape and size, in fact, the less you conform the better.

'Like Caramella and Oscar,' I say, and he says, 'Exactly.' And then he tells me a story about a boy who reminded him of Oscar. He's tall and awkward, this boy, and he can't do any tumbling, couldn't even do a back flip, so he had a lot of trouble fitting in with the other boys who were all tumblers and jugglers. But he persevered. He took up spinning bowls and he practised and practised and, because of his character, which was obsessive and kind of sad, not only did he get very good at it but he was always picked for the main shows, as the kind of tragic, comic circus figure, and his performances were always very good. So his confidence grew and grew and soon all the boys wanted to learn spinning bowls too. He's left the circus now, but he's still performing, and the spinning bowls legacy remains.

The more Ruben talks about the circus the more excited I become, and my old opinion about the absolute necessity of me becoming a circus star quickly re-lodges itself in my head again and then I begin to grow nervous, especially as the conversation veers towards my impending audition. Ruben starts to fill me in.

'There are actually two kinds of auditions going on. First there's a selection group of kids who do basic training on Saturdays. At the end of the year, those kids get to audition to become part of a training group. Once you are in a training group you join the circus, go to the circus school and begin full-time training. That's what Kite is in now.'

'How many are in that?'

'Somewhere between seventy and a hundred. But from that group there's another selection made for the show, so maybe forty kids, depending on what the show needs, will be chosen. That's what Kite will be auditioning for.'

'And I will be auditioning for the training group?'

'Yes. Now, because you're not part of the selection group, I've organised a private audition for you. That means the trainers will ask you to do certain things and judge whether you're up to the standard. Most kids here start training at the age of eight, so you'll be expected to be at the same level as the other kids who are your age and who have been training a lot longer, so it won't be easy, but its not impossible either.'

Ruben smiles, but maintains a serious tone. I can tell he doesn't want me to get my hopes up, and I can feel them sinking fast.

'So, I don't have to do any special act.'

'No, that's just for the training group. Kite might have been confused about that.'

I look at Kite. I'm thinking, All that time learning a skateboard trick for nothing.

Kite jumps in. 'But Cedar's as good as Frankie and all those other girls,' he says, as if he can tell I'm losing hope.

'Well, yes, her basic tumbling is and her natural ability might even be better, but what she doesn't have yet is the form, and she doesn't have a specialist skill.'

'What's that?' I say.

'Ah, form is just learning to point your toes and keep your legs straight. It's nothing,' says Kite, rolling his eyes, 'we have to do bloody dance classes for form.'

Ruben laughs.

'Kite's form isn't his strong point, either.'

'What's a specialist skill?'

'As well as learning basic skills, all kids have to specialise. It can be in trapeze or manipulation, or hoop or cloud swing, whatever you choose. Spinning bowls, even. But for you, I imagine some kind of aerials.'

'What about tumbling?'

'That's a basic skill. Everyone has to learn tumbling, even the jugglers.'

I feel my hopes unravelling and lying flat on a table like a dirty trampled-on ribbon.

Ruben looks at me like he's trying to loosen me up with his gaze, trying to get that ribbon flying. He says, 'But Cedar, the thing is, what you *do* have is the right kind of determination and courage, and also a lot of raw potential. I'm sure the trainers will see that. You have to go in there

knowing you've got a good chance. All you can do is give it
your best shot. Okay?'

I sigh a big long sigh.

'Okay.' I try to find my courage. Where does it go when
your fear starts flooding in? It's like a little rock that's been
submerged and you have to dive down deep to feel it sitting
there.

Kite reaches over and squeezes my hand. 'You'll be great.
Don't worry.'

I look at him and then I think, I want to be great
because I want him to believe I am. Will he still like me if
I'm not?

Chapter 30

My audition is the next evening, after training finishes.
I haven't actually told Kite and Ruben about the slightly
enormous complication of my mum not wanting to move to
Albury, or not even knowing I'm here at all, though by now
she will know, since Barnaby was going to ring her for me.
Boy, am I glad he's going to speak to her and not me.
Sometimes a big brother is an excellent thing to have.

In the morning, Kite and I are standing in a slab of
morning sun in the driveway, waiting for Ruben, who is
going to drop Kite at school first and then take me to the
circus. The circus kids have their own school, and different
classes go off at different times of the day to do their training
session. Kite says some kids also go and train after school.

'Does everyone get sick of each other?'

'Not really. It's more like one enormous family. Imagine
having a family that big. It's great, really.' Kite's reaching into
the apricot tree but I can see he's all lit up, eyes shining,
because he has a huge family now. Makes me think how all

his life he's never even had a brother or a sister, and I can imagine how exciting it must be to be surrounded now by hundreds of kids, all of them doing something so huge and exciting together. I smile at him and I take the apricot he offers me, but I feel my thoughts snaking around and hissing up because I want to be happy for him, I really do, but mostly I feel my own selfish fears rising up and getting ready to bite. He'll be swallowed up, I'm thinking, by that enormous, exciting, wonderful new family and will never again want to do dumb things like hedge walking in Brunswick with just me.

I sink my teeth into the apricot and I feel that opinion, the one that thinks, If I don't get in that circus family, too, my life will be over. I feel it growing harder and firmer, and now it begins to throb and beat through the whole of my body. I walk out onto the nature strip and I look up at the sky, which is confidently blue, and I try to breathe in its largeness, and while I am breathing Kite comes up behind me and for a moment I can just feel him standing close. I can almost feel the warmth from his skin. But then he moves beside me and throws a pip at the letterbox.

'Hey, don't be nervous about the audition tonight. Dad was just saying all that because he wants to toughen you up. But the trainers are nice, they're all ex-Fruities themselves. You'll be fine.'

I imagine I am full of sky; I take a deep, quick, inconspicuous breath and act like I'm stretching my arms and then I just say in a 'by the way, while I stretch my arms'

kind of a way, 'So what about your audition piece? I guess
you can't use me, if I'm not in the same auditions. I guess
you'll be using Lola after all.'

I want him to say of course he still wants to work with
me, but at the same time I don't want him to know I want
all that. I want to act like I'm not jealous and I'm not
putting any pressure on. He's still looking straight ahead.

'Yeah. I kind of had no choice in the end. 'Cause we've
had to start rehearsing our pieces two weeks ago. So I had to
work with Lola. It's a pity, but I couldn't help it.'

'That's okay, I don't mind,' I say.

He looks at me as if he's trying to see if I do mind, so I
stare down at the ground as if I'm looking at the stones. And
just to be convincing, I bend down, pick one up and begin
to turn it over in my hand. Luckily, Ruben comes out right
then and hurries us into the car, because I don't think I
could hide my disappointment if I had to speak.

Kite's in the back of the car, so we don't even look at
each other all the way there. But by the time we drop Kite
at the school I'm almost wishing I hadn't come. I stare sadly
out the window and wonder if Kite loves me at all.

Ruben says, 'I got a call from your mother.'

'Oh.' I look down at my thin knees.

'Last night,' says Ruben. 'She just wanted to make sure
you were all right.'

'Ahh-huh.' I'm still looking at my knees and they haven't
changed.

'I told her you were fine.'

'That's good.'

Ruben reaches out and rubs my head. 'Little scamp!'

'Was she mad?'

'No. Just worried. She's all right, she says to say good luck.'

'Really?' Now I turn towards him, eyes bulging. I can hardly believe it. All of a sudden I feel my ribbon flying. All of a sudden the sky inside me lifts up and spreads out and I feel lighter and lighter, as if I might just waft out the window. I didn't realise how much it was weighing me down, not having my mum behind me. Suddenly, I feel infinitely better. I look at Ruben and he looks at me, and between us there's a flash of knowing. He smiles because he knows I ran away but he understands why, and maybe he would have done the same thing once. I smile because I know somehow he would have made Mum understand that too.

'Well, we're here,' he says, pulling into a small car park.

And there it is. A long, rectangular brick building painted white with bright red and orange and yellow strips of brick. At the top a sign which says:

THE FLYING FRUIT FLY CIRCUS

Instantly I am nervous again. It all seems so close, dangerously close. I close my eyes, I reach down into myself,

I say, 'Please, please let me join the circus.' I don't know who I'm asking. Just whatever it is out there that answers prayers. I know some people call it God, but because I'm unusual I might call it something else, like Janet, for instance. But right now I'm following Ruben inside, and I'm too excited to choose names for the Holy Spirit.

Chapter 31

Inside, first there is a hallway lined with posters and photos, and then it opens up into a place with bright coloured benches. On one side there's an office and a kitchen, and on the other a yellow change room and toilets, but best of all is what's in front. To me it looks like a long, long, wide hall of heaven. Shiny wood floors covered in acromats, crash mats, trampets, vaults, unicycles, hoops. At the end there's a circus curtain, and coloured rectangles of brick on the walls, like the outside. Hanging in the air are cloud swings, trapezes, webs, hoops and other things I don't know the names of. And what's most exciting of all is the action: kids everywhere, climbing up ropes, swinging in the air, somersaulting off the mini-tramps, tossing batons and burning round on unicycles.

As we walk in, two small girls in purple T-shirts, silver sparkly top hats and moustaches and glasses rush up to Ruben, grinning.

'Hi Ruben.'

'Nice moustaches,' he says, and they giggle and rush back off.

'They're all practising for the auditions,' he says to me. 'Those two are doing a double act on the trapeze.'

'Flying trapeze?' I say.

'No, just hanging. Too young for flying. They're only nine or ten.'

He sits me on a bench so I can watch, and introduces me to a young man who walks by wearing a blue singlet and a pink tissue crown, and then Ruben goes into his office for a while.

As I install myself, I really feel like I'm looking at my idea of the best party in the world. I feel my legs twitching to get out there, but I hold myself on the bench and I watch.

Right near me there's a young girl spinning on the web, which is a long rope hanging from the ceiling, and it has a small padded loop on the end that you can hang from, either by your ankle or your hand. Underneath her there's a trainer: a young woman in a black T-shirt with long messy hair, lying on her back on the crash mat and using the end of the rope to spin the web. The trainer is yelling out instructions to the girl up on the web.

'Hold your form, spin, don't use your hand, where's your hand spin? Don't you do it? There's room for it.'

Suddenly, some loud, heavy music comes on. There's a small red-headed boy in black trackies, fiddling with the CD player. He then gets on his unicycle and calls out to another boy who's older and who's juggling clubs.

'Hey, Adrian, you ready? Watch this!' Adrian catches his clubs and watches as the small boy tries to do an advancing twist on the unicycle. When he falls, they both laugh and Adrian starts up with his juggling. Adrian is standing on the acromat. Behind him and above there is an Indian girl going through a series of positions on a hanging hoop. A young woman strides out of the trainers' room and yells out towards the back of the room. She has a face like a pixie, and short, spiky brown hair.

'Rich, can you have a look at Guy's round-off somersaults? He's giving me a heart attack. They're this high!' She indicates with her hand. 'Get him to use his hands, for God's sake.'

Rich, who's the trainer with the pink tissue crown on, nods and leaves the kids on the mini-tramp to watch an older boy who is up the back on a long acromat. I try to watch him too, but then a girl about my age enters the hall from a side room. She's wearing a full white leotard and a trailing white silky scarf, which she keeps twirling and flicking. She has straight, thick, glossy hair tied in pigtails and, horror of all horrors, she's carrying a hoop.

My heart leaps.

Lola?

I know it's her. She reminds me of a pony. A special, rare white pony in a field of horses. A pony who never stumbles or gets muddy. She holds the hoop above her head and then lets it slide down her body, catching it with spinning hips. Ruben taps me on the shoulder.

'You all right here?'

'I'm fine.'

Standing next to him is the pixie woman.

'This is Sarah. She's our head trainer. She's one of the original Flying Fruit Flies.'

Sarah lets out a snort as if to say 'big deal', and then she grins at me.

'Hi, Cedar. I'm going to be auditioning you tonight, so Ruben thought I should just give you a rundown of what we'll be doing, and see if you have any questions.'

'Okay.' I budge over and she sits down next to me on the bench. Ruben bounces away to sit on the red vault and watch the training. Sarah tells me it will be just her and another trainer there, and that after a warm-up she'll test my strength and flexibility and then acrobatics. I tell her I haven't done any trapeze and she says it doesn't matter. She asks me if I can hold a handstand. I nod.

'You'll be fine.'

I note that everyone is telling me how I'll be fine. Maybe it's a clue, I think. I don't ask her any questions and after a while her attention drifts out to the hall, and she stands up and claps her hands at the girl on the cloud swing.

'Hey, Alex, in between tricks you get like this.' She makes her body all floppy. 'You have to be nice the whole way. Think about where your toes are. Keep your legs nice.'

Form, I think, that's what form is. When I can, I quickly turn my attention back to Lola, but she's disappeared, as all mysterious and alluring white ponies do. Instead, there's a girl on stilts with long shiny blue pants, twirling her arms to Kate Bush singing 'Babushka'. Her arms, I'm thinking, as if I've suddenly become a trainer myself, aren't always 'nice'. Sarah suddenly plonks herself down beside me again. She looks at her watch.

'This session will end at twelve, and the next group don't arrive till after lunch, so, if you want to, you can go eat your lunch now and use the acromat during the break. Mish and Frankie might be in here with me for some trapeze, so I can supervise.'

She taps my leg and smiles. 'Not that you need supervision, it's just the rules here. No one's allowed to train without a trainer on the floor.'

She hops up again and says, 'Excuse me, that's Mr Lee's sister; she's a new trainer here.' She points to an old Chinese woman who has just entered.

I'm not quite ready to leave yet. For one thing, I want to wait and see if Lola appears, but also, I'm still watching and it's making me excited. Who needs lunch, I think, when you're sitting at the gates of heaven?

Chapter 32

I am still sitting there at lunchtime when Frankie (who turns out to be a girl with a boy's name) and Mish come in to run through audition pieces with Sarah. They're both about my age. Mish comes in wearing a white leotard with a short fluorescent pink skirt. She's small and compact, and she's stuffing some kind of muesli bar down her throat before she starts stretching out on the acromat. Frankie is laughing loudly and swinging her suntanned arms, which all at once seem strong and soft. She's got those kind of eyes that crinkle up and shine so her face gets taken over by cheek. She's wearing a bright bold blue singlet and knee-length black leggings. She flashes an inquiring grin at me.

'I'm Frankie,' she says, sitting down opposite and taking off her sneakers.

'I'm Cedar.'

'Oh, you're Kite's friend?'

'Yep.'

'Well, we all love Kite here. Hey Mish, this is Cedar, Kite's friend.'

Mish lifts her head from the acromat and waves.

'You're auditioning, aren't you?' says Frankie. She's pulling on some kind of leather pads over her ankles.

'Yeah,' I blush a bit. I'm embarrassed to admit it. I feel like they might be scornful; they might think I'm an upstart.

'It'd be great if you get in. Good luck,' she says, and her eyes are sparkling at me.

'Thanks.' I feel shy in front of her because she seems entirely comfortable, like if she was a tree she'd be a very strong, shining, happy big one. Maybe she'd be that spreading elm tree on Punt Rd, the one I'd like to become.

'How long have you been in the circus?' I say.

'Since I was eight. Me and my friend Elsie joined at the same time. But lots of kids come in older. Have you met Matthew?' She nods her head in the direction of a tall, thin, freckly boy who's trying to balance a red bucket on his nose while juggling clubs.

'Matt,' she yells at him, 'come and meet Cedar.'

Matthew drops his head, lets the bucket fall into his hands and lifts his nose towards us, squinting. Then he nods and lopes over, with a club in each hand. He looks awkward.

'Hi,' he says. Frankie takes over.

'Tell her how you joined. She's auditioning. Tell her what a great family we are, so she feels welcome.' Frankie leans her head back and lets out that loud peal of laughter again as she wanders out to the mat to warm up.

Matthew is wearing a big baggy black T-shirt. He sticks a

finger in his ear and scrunches up his face as if he's not sure what to do. So I start.

'How long have you been in the circus?'

'Two years. I was fourteen when I came.'

'I'm thirteen.'

'Yeah? Well it's great here. Changed my life.'

'Are you a tumbler?'

'Nah. They're trying to teach me. You have to learn it, but I'm so stiff. I'm a juggler. Taught myself in my bedroom while I was at school.'

'Did you go to school in Melbourne?'

'No, I'm from Sydney. But hated school. See, I had a lisp. So I was bullied. I found out about this circus, wrote to them, sent them a video, and now I board here with another family.'

'Doesn't your mum mind?'

'A bit. But she's glad because I'm happy. I'm much more confident now. I used to be shy of being myself. Now I am myself. 'Cause people here appreciate you. Back home, no one appreciated a bedroom juggler.'

'Yeah, right. I can imagine. I was a closet cartwheeler.' He laughs at this, and because I've already asked too many questions I don't ask another, and since he doesn't ask me anything we both start watching Mish, who's on the flying trapeze. She's wearing a harness, and Sarah's holding the other end. She's swinging it high, and then she drops off backwards and hangs from her knees. I love the noise it makes, the whoosh and the thump when she drops. It's all so dramatic.

'Oh, she's good!' I say.

'Yeah. But you wait till you see Frankie. She's the best.'

Obviously, I think to myself, I'm not the only one to notice Frankie's star quality. Matthew picks up his clubs and wanders back over to pick up his bucket trick. I watch him for a minute, thinking how he looks like an ordinary guy but the thing is, he's not. He's doing something brave, and he's doing it himself. He's made his own decision and he's determined. I watch that bucket fall off his nose three times and each time he catches it, props it back up and starts juggling again.

When Frankie climbs up the rope for her routine, I watch the whole thing. Matthew is right of course; she seems to fly higher, float longer and flow through tricks effortlessly. There's one crazy thing she does where she tries a huge upside-down twist in the air and the first time she falls, though the harness suspends her in mid-air and Sarah goes flying up because she's the weight on the other end of the rope. The second time, Sarah's yelling out, 'Feet, feet,' but Frankie gets it. Mish claps. Someone else whistles.

'Boy, what's that called?' I ask Mish.

'It's a hocks, full twist to clicks. Clicks is where you hang from your feet.'

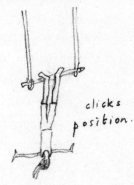

clicks position.

'Looks hard.'

'Only Frankie can do it.'

'Doesn't it hurt, to catch yourself with your feet like that?'

'Kills. But you get used to it.' She points to her feet and shins. They're bruised and red. I let out a sympathetic breath.

'Ouch. Still, must be fun.'

'It's the best. You'll love it.'

I smile at her. One thing's clear, I think, as I wander out to find some lunch, no one here seems to be one bit protective or exclusive, or even snobby. That sure makes me feel good. Though, I guess I haven't really met Lola yet.

Chapter 33

I decide I won't go back for the afternoon session. For one
thing, I know that's when Kite will be training and I don't
want to be there, gawking from the sidelines, watching him
and Lola do their adagio. Also, I figure I need to just settle
my mind down (it's all in a flap) and empty some of it out
(it's a bit overloaded).

There's the river over the road and a big park with
swirling paths lined with plane trees. I take my sandwich and
lie down under a tree whose leaves are wiggling and
fluttering in the air, just like my thoughts. Strangely, I find
myself thinking about what Barnaby said in the car to Ada,
about me being attracted to the glamour and not thinking
our own circus is a real circus. I figure by then he knew I
was there, so really he was saying it for my benefit.
Immediately I want to say to him, 'Bruised shins aren't
glamorous.' But then I think to myself, in my eyes they are;
there's nothing I want more than red ankles and bruised
shins. I know they don't look good in a frock, but I like

them because they're extreme. They're wounds gathered in the pursuit of something extraordinary – flying through the air. To me that's glamour. Or something special. And what's wrong with wanting that?

I don't answer that thought because I'm thinking about The Acrobrats. I'm thinking about Oscar and Caramella, and Inisiya and Nidal, and even Mohammed with his sad, serious face. Then I think, that's the dirt. It's real. It's like earth, it's not shining or wrapped up or stunning. It's different from flying in the air. It's about making something on the ground, slowly, undramatically, quietly, like a builder builds a house, like a beetle carrying one crumb back to his beetle house.

I close my eyes and try to clear both feelings from my head, because they're tugging at each other. There's one thing I know for sure and it's that I have to grab this opportunity to fly, because if I don't I'll forever and forever regret it. I don't think regret would suit me, not one bit. So I open my eyes, stare up at the leaves and ask the blue heavens to let me be as fine as everyone says I'll be.

Chapter 34

My audition is at five-thirty. I turn up an hour earlier,
thinking I might just find some empty acromat to roll
around on, or at least I might gather some encouragement
from Kite or Ruben.

Kite is there. He's not training though, he's lying on an
acromat on his tummy and Lola is standing on him. She's
still in her floaty white outfit and she's giggling and treading
up his back. He's making low moaning appreciative sounds,
as if he's really liking it. He can't see me because his head is
turned to the side. I immediately feel as if I should leave, as
if I'm intruding, or as if that writhing jealous feeling might
make itself so obvious that people will look at me and see a
twisting red smoke flame out my nostrils. But as I turn
around to begin my escape, Frankie yells out to me.

'Hey, Cedar, I'm glad you're back. Do you want me to
show you some trapeze?'

Kite flips his head towards me, grins and puts his hands to
the floor as if to push up. Lola stops giggling and flicks her

head to stare at me. We lock eyes only for a second before I look away and reply to Frankie, who's like an angel, swinging gently above us on her perch.

'Okay. Thanks. I'd love to try some trapeze.'

'She can't do that Frank, she's got her audition in a minute. She'll get too tired. You'll wreck her hands.' Kite's getting up off the floor and coming towards me. He nods at Lola and says, 'Cedar, come and meet Lola.'

Lola by now is smiling and tilting her head to one side while stretching her arms behind her head, and she looks very elegant and almost as if someone has styled her for a photograph.

'Hi,' she says.

'Hi,' I say back. She keeps smiling, but releases her arms and begins slowly rolling her shoulders.

'Lola was just giving me a back massage with her feet,' says Kite. 'You should try it, Cedar, it's great.'

'How did your rehearsal go?' I say. (As if I want Lola walking on my back!)

'Great. How was your day?'

'Fine.' I feel as if both Frankie, swinging above us, and Lola, who has elegantly sunk to the floor and is stretching out in a twist, are watching us. Frankie from above and Lola from below. It's suddenly as if Kite and I hardly know each other and the air between us has stiffened like some freshly starched sheet that everyone can see. Frankie laughs and begins swinging vigorously.

'Come on, Kite, let her try a little trapeze, I know she'll love it.'

'Yeah,' says Lola, perching herself up on her delicate elbows. 'Let her try. She's only got to do a few cartwheels for the audition.'

Suddenly I feel as if the ground I was standing on just fell away and I'm paddling like a dog through a tide of opinions, and not sure where the snags are. Kite looks directly at me, anchors me with his soft brown eyes.

'It's up to Cedar. What do you want to do, Cedar?'

I stare wildly back at him as if he might have the answer. It's as if I'm sensing something but I don't know what it is. I feel like an animal that might be about to walk into a trap or a dangerous situation, and my nose is twitching. It's not that I'm afraid of the trapeze, it's something else; it's just a sixth sense thing, a twilight zone moment in which I look suddenly at Lola.

'Do you do trapeze?'

'I do hoop.'

'Lola doesn't like heights,' calls out Frankie as she unwinds herself and hops off.

'Kite does, though.' Frankie is looking at Kite and laughing again. Lola picks up a hoop and starts flicking it. I suddenly pipe up.

'You know what? I think I'll just warm up right now.' I have to trust my one clear feeling, which is that I don't want to be on show, I don't want to enter the game. I'm not sure what the game is and who's set up the rules, but one thing I do know: I don't like games with strategies – I only like Snap. Whatever the thing is that I sense with Lola, Frankie, Kite and the trapeze, I don't have to be in it. I can just quietly do what I know I'm here to do, and it isn't to show anybody whether I can or can't do trapeze; not Frankie, not Lola and not even Kite.

Frankie just nods, smiling, and Lola ignores me altogether. Although it seems to me that I've made some monumental decision, no one seems to be too affected by it, and no one pats me on the back and says, 'Well done,' not even Kite.

I look up at the gently swinging trapeze almost longingly. Have I just missed my one chance to show them all what a flyer I could be? The trapeze says nothing, but continues to swing tauntingly, though this is what I hear it saying, 'Cedar, if you want to fly you will fly your own way, not someone else's way.'

I sigh because the trapeze is wise and it knows me well, and I think to myself, I must remember to tell Aunt Squeezy about this fine decision because it will give me a good score in my Buddhist training.

Sarah comes out of her office, claps her hands together and tells the others to go home and let me centre myself for five minutes. As they leave, Frankie yells out, 'Good luck Cedar!' and Kite just winks and says, 'I'll wait outside for you.' Lola has managed to slip out with a small flick of her pigtails. Seems like a long five minutes that I'm alone on the acromat, and I lie there on my back and try to feel the ground holding me up. I close my eyes and try to focus my thoughts on the ground, but I can hear the gentle creak of the trapeze and it seems to be squeaking at me, and I think how whenever I'm on the ground it's the air that draws me up, but once I'm in the air, it's the ground that I need to return to. Maybe life is not about one or the other but the way you move between them. I like this thought, but just as I'm about to develop it, Sarah steps out onto the mat and says,

'Shall we start warming you up? You ready?'

Chapter 35

To tell you the truth, the audition was nothing to talk about. No lights, no beautiful breathtaking moments, just me doing what Sarah said. A dive roll, a dive roll to a handstand, a back roll, cartwheel, a round-off, a round-off to a back flip. I said I couldn't do this, but I could do a back walk-over. There were flexibility and strength tests and then a few questions and it was over. Sarah said she'd let me know, but she didn't give me a clue, not even with her expression, which remained sharp and friendly the whole way.

That night, Kite and Ruben and I go down to the Termo to see Barnaby and Ada playing. This is almost as good as the night I imagined with the Argentinean tango teacher, and luckily I don't need a lava lamp or a frock.

The Termo is a big old pub opposite the train station. Inside, where Barnaby is playing, it's dark and smoky and crowded. I'm not sure why, but I feel excited. Maybe it's the darkness; maybe it's being out with Kite in a grown-up place; maybe it's because I've done the audition and now

I can relax; or maybe it's because I feel special since all the people are here to see my brother and I can shine with the borrowed light of his specialness.

But mostly I think it's because Kite holds my hand. No one can see we're holding hands because everyone is standing up and it's so crowded. I lean into Kite a little. I can do this because it's what people do when bodies are all messy and together and covered in darkness and anticipation. Ruben is standing at the back, but we've pushed through into the middle of the crowd. Barnaby and Ada aren't the main act: they're supporting The Vines, but still, standing up there together, with electric guitars, they look like a real thing, a real act, not just Barnaby and Ada but something else. It's like the music transforms them. Just like the trapeze transforms Frankie.

Ada looks out from her long black hair and holds the microphone in one hand. She says in a low, slow voice, 'This one's for our friend, the stowaway.'

Barnaby is grinning and looking out in the crowd and I know he is looking to see me. At this moment I feel as if I could just be dancing tango in a gorgeous frock, but I hold the feeling inside me and all I do is lean a little more into Kite and grin, and right then I know I'm having a moment of perfect happiness. If only Lola could see me now, she'd know I wasn't afraid of heights, not one bit.

We have to leave before the end because it's late, but I don't mind since I'm just not in the mood for minding anything. When we get home, Ruben shuffles off inside and Kite plonks himself down on the verandah steps and pulls me down beside him, saying, 'Sit down and look at the sky, it's different here. The stars are brighter and the night is blacker.'

I'm smiling at the stars and at the night and at the feeling inside me, which is brighter than the stars and bigger than the night. Before it happens, it's as if I know it will. But I turn to Kite and I'm nervous and he looks at me and very slowly our faces begin to touch and we kiss. Not just one kiss, but two,

then three,

then four.

All soft, long kisses, all getting longer and closer, and closer. And then our mouths are opening, and slowly we're kissing a real grown-up kiss.

On the steps, under the night.

Kite and me.

Chapter 36

Next day, I'm catching the train back to Melbourne. It's been arranged. Ruben drops Kite at school then takes me to the train station, but I'm not too sad to say goodbye this time because not only have I been well and truly kissed, I've a good feeling I'll be back to join the circus. Ruben says he'll be ringing me in the next couple of days to let me know.

It's only as I'm saying goodbye to Ruben that I suddenly remember Harold Barton's letter. I'd been so distracted by my own excitement that I'd forgotten all about it.

Ruben reads it right there on the platform. He raises his eyebrows as he reads and then looks at me, surprised.

'Did you know what this was about?'

'No.' I begin to feel worried.

'He wants to join the circus.'

'Harold Barton!' I couldn't believe it. 'Harold Barton wants to join the circus? How? I mean, what does he do?'

'Apparently he juggles. He says here he can do tennis and other tricks.'

'He never told me that.'

'No. Well, I think the lad holds his cards quite close.'

'What do you mean?'

'I mean there's quite a lot you wouldn't know about Harold Barton because he hides it, but he's had a tough time.'

'A hard time? I thought he had it easy. He looks like he does.'

'Yeah. I know he gets lots of things. His parents spend money on him because they feel guilty they don't get on; in fact I think they're estranged. His dad is a difficult man. Very troubled. I don't think he's really able to father Harold at all. In fact the circus would probably be very good for Harold. Why don't you tell him to give me a call?'

'Is his father mean to him?'

'I don't know exactly what goes on. I just know it's a difficult home life for Harold. He's not as tough as he seems.'

All of a sudden there's a lot of things I want to ask Ruben because I have a feeling he knows stuff, I mean the underneath stuff, the great lurking realness. But my train has arrived and he's ushering me towards it. For one thing, I'm wondering how he knows all that about Harold. Has he spoken to Harold? I even remember once Harold asking me about my dad and I wasn't being very friendly because I always assume with Harold that I have to be ready for an attack. Maybe Harold really wanted to talk. Poor Harold, I think to myself, and it almost shocks me to have a sympathetic thought for Harold Barton.

But I'm happy to wriggle into my seat on the train because I can sense a bit of thinking coming on and there's nothing better than a train ride for getting the mind in a loose and rambling mood. Before I even start on Harold Barton, I want to go over the night before's spectacular kissing event.

I stare out the train window and immediately plunge down like a deep-sea diver into my memory of it and swim in a floating, winding way through the words and feelings and moments as if they are a strange shimmering wonderland. But somewhere in the wonderland there's an awkward and unexpected bend, something I can't just glide through or know how to negotiate. It comes after the kiss which, of course, eventually stopped, since everything does have to stop some time, or at least change and become something else, even though there are some moments you want to just keep going on and on. I don't know how it stopped, I just remember Kite looking at me and I think our eyes were still kissing, or if eyes had hands then our eyes were holding each other, and Kite said, 'Hey, I really like you, Cedar.'

I didn't say anything, except I smiled and kissed him right on the soft spot near his eye. I don't know why I didn't say anything; maybe I didn't want to just copy or follow. Instead, I looked down at our hands, which were wound up together. And then Kite stood up, heaving me up with him. He led me inside, and that's when we came to the hard corner. He took me to his bedroom.

At the door he turned towards me.

I said, 'Where are we going?'

It was obvious of course, but I'd begun to feel like everything was getting deep way too fast and I needed a moment to work out where I was.

He grinned and whispered, 'Come and lie on my bed,' and I grinned too, because what could be better than to kiss and press your whole body close all at once?

But what if things went even further? What if he put his hand up my shirt and discovered I had only small boobs? What if he didn't like me anymore after that? Maybe he'd only just decided he did like me and I didn't want him to change his mind now. But if I didn't go and lie on his bed, would he think I was a boring old prude? In fact, was I being a boring old prude? Was I being backward? I breathed in. Come on, Cedar, I said to myself. If someone's going to love you, they have to know you, small boobs and all.

'Okay,' I said, just like that, just because I didn't want to be a scaredy cat. And just as we began to plunge into the bedroom, Ruben emerged from the bathroom in his blue spot pyjamas and we all stopped moving and stood there in the hall, trapped in this feeling that Ruben had just caught us out, and even Ruben didn't know quite how to act or what to say. The first thing that happened was Kite let my hand drop and Ruben smiled softly and coughed and said he thought we should both be in our *own* beds by now, and he looked at Kite and said he'd assured my mother that he'd

take good care of me while I was staying with him. Kite just
grinned and turned me by the shoulders towards my room.

'She was just on her way,' he said.

'Good night,' I said, and off I scurried, leaving them to
sort out their father and son stuff in the hall.

Once I got into my own bed I wasn't sure if I was
relieved or disappointed, and even now, as the train chugs
along, I can't work it out.

When you really, really want someone to like you, you do
everything you can to make yourself likeable. Some people,
like Marnie, put on make-up to look more appealing.
Others, like Harold Barton, flash their new enviable things
around, as if those things are extra limbs of themselves.
Whereas someone like Caramella has the opposite strategy.
She tries always to deflect attention away from herself by
wearing big T-shirts and by being always more interested in
you.

It's normal to hide your real self away under make-up, or
shirts, or with things or diversions. My way of making myself
likeable is to put on an act. With Kite, I act like I'm not
jealous or like I'm not scared, and last night I was even
prepared to act like I'm not shy about certain possible
physical things that could happen between a boy and a girl,
when really I am. I'm very shy, actually.

So, what happens if you make a boy like you, but it's the
other carefully constructed version of you that he likes; the
one with lipstick on, or the one with the Wonder Bra, or the

one with the bold, brave, easygoing, very cool act? What
happens if he likes *that* you and not the real you, the shy,
uncertain you? How long can you keep wearing your
lipstick? How long can you hide the real you?

And if boys do it too, what version of Kite am I in love
with anyway? What is he hiding from me? Is he really as
great as I think he is? For instance, just because he kisses me
doesn't mean he isn't kissing Lola as well. When I think
about it, Kite sure doesn't give much of himself over. We've
never even spoken together about feelings, or us, and that's
because I can tell he wouldn't like to speak, so I make it easy
for him to keep himself to himself. But, come to think of it,
what I really want is to sit down and talk without hiding or
pretending or putting on an act.

It's not as easy as you think to be yourself, and I mean
your true, quaking, bumpy, hurtable, hungry self. Maybe
what you really are is just a shape, like this:

which is always changing, always aiming to become

a more defined and certain spectacular shape like this:

though really what you need to become is just more comfortable with the shape that you are:

because even that shape will keep changing:

and changing:

Chapter 37

Aunt Squeezy picks me up from the train station because Mum is at work. She's waiting there on the platform at Spencer Street when I get off, leaning up against a wall with that faraway gaze in her eyes. She looks small and dusty and swallowed by the concrete platform, but she seems to me like a quiet, inspired dab of colour on a hard, grey ground. Aunt Squeezy always wears clothes that float and dangle and waft around her in layers of washed-out colours. I like the way she seems oblivious to fashion. When I land at her feet she jumps out of her dreaming, grins and gives me a big hug. I'm so glad to see her I begin instantly telling her all about my adventure, being sure not to leave out the bit about the wise moment with the trapeze. Then she starts telling me all about her adventure, only hers is a lot longer. She left home when she was only seventeen, and has been travelling ever since.

'Why didn't you go back?' I say.

She sighs. 'I never got on well with my parents.'

'Oh, there's a bit of that going around,' I say, thinking of Harold Barton.

She laughs because she thinks I'm talking about my own mum.

'Hey, your mum's not mad at you. She was really understanding. You're lucky to have a mum like that. I think when I arrived in your family I was hoping I'd kind of join up, and your mum's been so welcoming. But I've decided to go home now.'

'*What?* You can't go home now. You *have* joined up. You'd be deserting us. Besides, I don't want you to go.' My head is suddenly reeling or rising up on its hind legs like a horse. Maybe it's already a bit tightly wired with all my own new feelings and hopes, and this comes like a big, final blast to the circuitry.

Aunt Squeezy smiles in her softening way. 'I'd love to stay. But you know how you were saying about being brave and true? Well, I think I need to be brave now and clear up things with my mum before I become a mum myself. I have to at least try, anyway.'

'No you don't,' I say petulantly.

Aunt Squeezy puts her hands on her tummy, which is beginning to stick out. 'It's not just that. It's also this feeling I'm getting about needing to grow up now. Now I'm going to be responsible for someone else, I can't just keep travelling around and leading my own life. You'll understand what I mean when you have a baby.'

'I won't have a baby, then. I always want to lead my own life.'

She laughs again and her owl eyes shine as if she's just seeing a brand new thing in the field. 'Oh, Cedar, you're so like me. Or I was just like you at your age. That's going to be good for us. I think we'll always understand each other.'

She throws her arm around me. 'Don't worry, I'll stay in touch. I may even be back – who knows.'

'You better move back. You're going to need a babysitter,' I say. And, for the first time ever, I think I almost know what it must be like to have an older sister. I feel close to Aunt Squeezy in a way that's different from the way I feel about Caramella. It's not better, it's just as if Aunt Squeezy and I are two odd red flowers off the same bush, whereas Caramella and I come from very different bushes. Caramella and I have such different ways that it's interesting, it's slanted and far-ranging. What Aunt Squeezy and I have is just a knowing, a plain enduring home-baked knowing that comes out of the simple fact that we grew on the same bush. I feel really good and proud and bouncy as I walk down the street with Aunt Squeezy, just as if we were sisters. I feel almost like it doesn't matter that she's leaving; what matters is that she came and now my family is bigger.

So, when we get home and the phone rings I'm completely unprepared for it to be Ruben and even less prepared for him to say, 'Cedar, I'm sorry to have to tell you that you didn't get selected for the circus.'

Chapter 38

It's all very well to live your own life, but what happens when your life doesn't want to live you? How do you cope when your life swerves off the course you so determinedly set it on? I felt cheated. I felt that God had just come along and scribbled all over my master plan, and now I no longer had a trail to go along. Before the phone call I'd had a bursting, wriggling, burning line of hopes that were leading me onwards, and now someone or something had erased that line completely and I couldn't go on without it. My life was rubbed out.

'You're being too dramatic,' says Mum, while I am still sobbing on my bed. 'Your life hasn't been rubbed out at all. I work with people whose lives really have been rubbed out, and you're not one of them. You're alive and well, just very disappointed, but you'll get over it, I promise you will. It's a feeling, and it will go. We all have to feel disappointment along the way – it's part of life.'

She has a point. She has a couple actually. Firstly the old

'there's-always-someone-worse-off-than-you point' which, frankly, I think is a bit unfair because I don't want to make myself look better by comparing my misfortunes to greater misfortunes. It doesn't seem right. Feels like you are treading on someone whose face is already in the mud, just so you can get a foot-up. But then there's also the unbearable fact that disappointment is part of life.

'That doesn't mean you have to like it!'

I lift my head up from the bed. She smiles and gently pushes the hair off my face.

'No, it's rotten when it comes, but you have to be ready to let it go and move on as well.'

Move on? That was exactly the problem. Where? Now I'd never see Kite and he'd run off for ever and my whole career as world-touring acrobat would be over. I stop sobbing as I pause to wonder which is worse: the loss of Kite, or the loss of career.

As if hearing my thoughts, Mum says, 'Anyway, you mustn't think of it as the end. There are always other opportunities, and you'll find them. If anyone can find an opportunity, you can.'

I shake my head dismally, mainly because I'm just feeling feeble and shaky and don't even want to look past the place where my life has stopped.

Aunt Squeezy, of course, takes a similar approach: that same character-building line of reasoning. She even says, 'Don't worry, losers are much more interesting people than winners.'

I'm appalled. 'Are you saying I'm a loser?'

'No, no, I'm just saying now you've had the experience of losing something you wanted. That's a great opportunity life has presented you with.'

'I would have preferred the opportunity of touring the world in a circus.'

'Sure, but this doesn't mean you don't get that opportunity, it just means you have to work harder for it. You have to trust, now, that there's a good reason. You just can't see it yet.'

It isn't until the early evening that I eventually drag myself up off my bed. I take Stinky down the creek. The sun is sinking and the trees are sighing in relief. It's been a slow, hot day, but now the shadows are long and the air has loosened and the sky has relinquished its relentless blue hold and let a dirty pink flush creep in. I sigh too. It seems that something is giving way. Not just the long, hot day of sobbing, but my holding on to it. I even notice a little glad thought, like the short pealing song of a bird sheltering in the shade. As I watch Stinky's hairy bum happily trotting towards the creek, I think that at least I won't have to live away from him now. Or Mum. And even Barnaby.

And then I begin to try to think about what Ruben had said on the phone, about how it was between me and one other girl and we were both as good as each other, only since she'd been training with the circus group she'd learned a specialist skill. That was the only difference. So I was very, very close, and there'd be more auditions next year.

Next year, I thought to myself, would I still want it? And just as I wondered this I walked onto the bridge and saw a wobbly, trickling line of rocks wrapped in blue, spreading down the bank.

Oscar's rocks.

It quite stopped me, hushed my thoughts, because it kind of asked you to look at it. To smile at it. This quiet tumble of blue looked like a moment caught and offered, like a spectacular sentence basking on a sunny ledge, unaware of its own significance. There was a whole bank of rocks, but simply by being wrapped in bits of blue — old shabby blue T-shirt, used tea towels, a blue curtain — a procession of them had been transformed into royalty, into something that was majestic in a home-made way. Just by standing out from the rest, they looked special, even though they were dressed in rags. Maybe also because they were a team; all of them together, holding their heads high and laughing down the hill.

The Acrobrats.

I thought of them, our new team of refugees. Their acrobatic skills were as shabby as those old blue rags, but they were a special team. They stood out like those blue rocks because they were different from the rocks they'd found themselves amidst. They had different cultures and histories and languages and experiences. It was as if they'd been plucked out of their land of blue rocks and plonked in a land of mud-coloured rocks. The Acrobrats might never be able to do back flips, but they were always going to have a story to tell.

I felt like rushing over to Oscar's house and telling him, because there's this thing about Oscar: I never know if he knows how much he knows, or if he just senses things but doesn't need to explain them, not even to himself. He just makes pictures or poems of things that reveal his own unique Oscar way. I felt like saying, 'Hey Oscar, I get it now, I get the rocks.' But I'm not sure he'd like it explained in words. I think he wouldn't like it worked out as if it was a riddle rather than the mysterious, beautiful thing that it is.

What's more, when I think of Oscar I feel ashamed of my misery. He's someone whose life was once partly rubbed out in a huge and forever way, and yet he's never given up. He goes on with his brain injury; goes on with more courage than I have. What would he think of me if he knew how I thought my life was over just because I didn't get selected? Oscar wouldn't think anything. He'd probably just laugh and clap his knee.

Chapter 39

As far as I knew, Caramella and Oscar didn't know about my three-day tragic adventure to Albury, and since I was back in time for Acrobrat training there was no reason to tell them – except that I felt I had to. Otherwise, I'd be hiding something from them (not a little thing but a rather huge thing), and it would be like trying to build a house together while not telling them that some of the floorboards had holes. Let's face it, if there are holes, everyone who's in the room should know where they are.

So, before training I meet up with Caramella. We sit in the gutter outside her house. She has a new top on. It's a pale blue sleeveless T-shirt with a purple swirly drawing of Janis Joplin on it. I've never seen Caramella wear anything kind of rock'n'roll before, let alone without sleeves, so I can't help commenting.

'Hey, nice top.'

She smiles shyly. 'Thanks. It was a present. But I chose it.'

'A present, who from?'

'Just Mum and Dad. For my birthday.'

'It was your birthday? On the weekend?'

'Yeah. I rang you to see if you wanted to come to the city with us. We went to the gallery. But you were away.' She drops her face and sticks her hands under the T-shirt.

Oh boy, I think. What kind of friend am I?

'Caramella, I'm so sorry. I didn't know. I wanted to tell you I was going, but I was scared you'd think I was deserting you because I went up to Albury to audition for the Flying Fruit Flies. It was something I felt I had to do – '

Caramella interrupts me. 'Don't worry about it. I understand. Your Aunt Squeezy explained to me when I rang up. You know, if some great drawing school asked me to apply, I would too, no matter what was going on. So don't feel bad.'

I feel a great rush of relief, which makes me look up at the heavens and breathe out, then I turn to Caramella.

'You know Caramella, you're the best.'

She laughs and draws her knees in close under her chin.

'And you look great in that T-shirt.' I really mean that, because all of a sudden she looks more comfortable; more as if she's sitting in her own skin, as if it's a good place to be. And in the end that's what makes something good, the way you can like it or love it or accept it and wear it. She rocks back and forth, mouth on her knee, large eyes peeping over the little fleshy mountains of leg as if they're half hiding and half venturing out.

'You don't think I look fat?' she says, taking her mouth off her knee.

'Nope. You look sexy.'

'Really?'

'For sure.'

She smiles her famously sweet, beaming smile and I feel myself beaming back because that's what happens when Caramella beams; you can't help getting all warmed up by it. I think to myself, This is great, this is really great. Who would have thought I could feel so great just one day after my glorious failure?

As we make our way to training I tell her about how I didn't get selected; how I almost did, but I didn't.

She doesn't seem concerned. 'But you'll get in. You'll get in next time.' And she just grins like it's no big deal.

'Yeah,' I say, and I kind of go along with her and act just as if it is no big deal, and the funny thing is I almost believe it myself. Because when I look around, the neighbourhood looks okay: houses are sitting as they should, all higgledy-piggledy and solid and old, the sun is out and everything is beaming beneath it, and I'm walking along with Caramella, who's my best friend. So I puff myself up with the gleaming goodness of the day and I say, 'I kissed Kite.'

She opens her eyes wide and grins. 'I knew it! I knew you would.'

'It was a real kiss. Went for ages. On the steps.'

'So, you in love?'

'I guess so. I'm not sure if he is, though.'

'Why?'

'Well, for one thing, there's this other girl called Lola and they seem pretty close. I don't even know if something's going on or not. Also, I haven't heard from him since I found out I didn't get in.'

'That was only yesterday.'

'Still.'

'Why don't you just ask him? I mean about Lola. Ring him up and ask.'

'Yeah. Maybe.' I sigh. That would really be giving the game away. But then again, isn't that what I decided I wanted – to just talk straight?

When we get to the Network, Caramella goes and talks to Mohammed, who is sitting at a computer. I see her give him something. He doesn't smile, he just nods approvingly and looks at her with a serious, shy look, then pins it on the wall next to his picture of some Bollywood movie star. It's the drawing of him that she did.

In the hall, Inisiya and Nidal are already practising a bluebird. I can hear their shrieks and giggles before I even enter the room, and it makes me feel happy. Despite myself I feel happy to see them falling out of balance and laughing their heads off.

Chapter 40

After training, I tell Oscar that I saw his rocks and that they made me feel better about life.

'Did they inspire you with their blueness?' he asks, pitching his shaggy eyebrows at a startling angle. He's sitting on a chair, peeling an orange, and looking quite deeply concerned.

'I'm not sure if it was the blueness or the togetherness or just the way something as ordinary as a blue tea towel transformed them, but whatever it is I think you're really great, Oscar. You're a transformer.'

'Why, thank you. I like to be a transformer.' He relaxes his brow and holds out a piece of orange for me, then frowns again. 'Can't seem to transform my handstands yet.'

It's true. It's unlikely that he'll ever be able to do a handstand, and yet he never gives up. I had always marvelled at how he kept trying and trying, even though it was useless. But right then it made sense because Oscar just didn't see it as impossible or even unlikely. For him, everything is always possible, even a handstand from someone who has trouble balancing on his two feet. That was what really made Oscar different. More than his brain injury, it was his belief in something other than what we know. He believed in something else; something beyond, some wild, invisible, shimmering possibility that sung out to him in the tones of magic.

'You will one day. I bet you'll transform the whole idea of what a handstand is,' I say.

'Yes,' he says. 'Of course, let's see. A handstand is a way of seeing the world tip upside-down. It's to clean the soles of your feet with air. It's a body's willing flip into unfamiliarity...' He begins to gesture broadly as if delivering a speech, and I laugh.

Seeing all the action, Caramella comes over. 'What's so funny?'

'Oh, just Oscar holding forth on handstands. But actually,' I say, 'there is something strange I need to tell you both.' With that I launch into the story of Harold Barton, including his hard life and his juggling ambitions.

Oscar says, 'I think it's magnificent. Harold Barton. A juggler.'

Caramella doesn't say anything for a while. She frowns and seems perplexed. Of course Harold Barton had always teased her a lot and called her Zit-face. She more than any of us would never want to trust him. After a while she says, 'Is he good? Can he really juggle?'

'I don't know, but I guess he must be okay because he knows all the names.'

She nods and says nothing more, at least not until we get home. The whole way there she's been quiet and thoughtful and I'm worried that I really disturbed her by bringing up the monstrous Harold Barton, so I try to reassure her by saying that if he did get into the Flying Fruit Fly Circus at least we wouldn't have to see him round here anymore.

'But I'm thinking about Mohammed,' she says, frowning and shaking her head.

'Mohammed?'

'Yes. This might be a crazy idea, but I was thinking that maybe Mohammed is scared of all the physical stuff in the circus. Maybe he's just not good at that stuff, like me. But juggling is something that boys can learn, isn't it?'

She looks at me with worry in her eyes, but I'm not sure what she's getting at. She finally says it. 'Couldn't we get Harold Barton to come to training to teach juggling?'

I stop dead still. So she's not scared of Harold Barton. She's even prepared to invite him in.

'God! It's a great idea, but wouldn't you hate that?'

'I'd put up with it.' She sighs and seems to relax, as if just saying it has given her the courage.

'You never know, it might transform Harold too,' I say, and I think to myself that transformation is obviously my new thing. That, and compassion. I give Caramella a hug.

'You know, Caramella, you're so forgiving, you're already a Buddhist, I think.' And then I go home to ring Harold and also to wait for Kite to call. Surely he'll call tonight.

Chapter 41

I ring Harold Barton, leave a message on his answering machine and then lounge around waiting for Kite to call. The first time the phone rings it's an Indian man trying to sell us a holiday to Noumea. Mum yells out, 'Tell him we can't afford the flights.'

Next it's Barnaby calling from a phone booth in Sydney. He doesn't get time to say much.

'Hello little lady, it's your big brother.'

'Hi, Barn, where are you?'

'Still in Sydney. How was the circus?'

'I didn't get in.'

'Hey, that's a bummer. Don't worry, I didn't get into the first band I auditioned for, either.'

'Didn't you?'

'Nah. You get over it. It's all part of the game. Now, can you tell Mum I'm okay. Safe and sound and all that. Leaving tomorrow.'

'So, how's Ada? You know I like her more now.'

'Yeah, so do I.'

'And guess what: Aunt Squeezy's leaving.'

'Why?'

The phone cuts off. I listen for a minute, wondering if that's how I would sound if you listened to my heart right now, then Mum calls out, 'Did he blow the head gasket?'

'No, he said he's coming home tomorrow.'

Mum sighs. She's lying on the couch with a green facemask on. I sit around drawing animals all over the phone pad and thinking how Kite can't really be thinking about me if he doesn't ring, and sometimes I wish I was a giraffe instead of a girl, because giraffes don't have boyfriends. Then I write *Cedar B. Freeman* to see how it looks, and then I write *Lola Freeman*, just to be mean to myself. And then finally I go to bed and dream that Aunt Squeezy gives birth to a giant poo.

✳

giraffe standing on a head gasket
and trying to eat a star.

Chapter 42

That week passes by without a call from Kite or even from Harold Barton, and I struggle through it as if the days are solid and thick and hard to push through. By the time Acrobrats' training arrives I feel weary in the head from all that wondering and worrying and pushing through. If you have a line of worry going on and then you weave your wonder through it, like this:

then your worry gets lured in by the wonder and starts to wind and wiggle and expand all over your thinking space, like this:

So this is what I looked like by the time I turned up for training:

And guess who was the first person I saw? Harold Barton slouching on the steps of the building with a bag at his feet.

'Hey,' I said, 'you showed up.'

'Guess so. Wasn't sure I'd come, but looks like I did.' He looks up, half-squinting and half-grinning at me.

'I'm glad you did,' I say nicely, because I remember how he's had a hard time at home, and I'm practising my compassion. While I'm standing there smiling at Harold Barton compassionately and he's looking at me like I've just turned into a baboon, Inisiya arrives and gives me a hug, and suddenly I feel a bit lighter, as if my expanding whirling worry lines just got rubbed out by all the warmth coming out and going in.

I introduce her to Harold Barton and she's sweet to him, just as if he's a regular lad, and the thing is he acts just as if he is a regular lad, and smiles at her and laughs in a friendly way as we make our way inside.

Caramella is already there, sitting on the floor with the Hmong girls, and I notice how there's something similar between them: a round softness, which makes them look like a circle of quiet little mushrooms. Especially compared to Sali from Sudan, who's already dive-rolling on the mat and yelling at Inisiya to come and hold a hoop. He's become known as 'Hopper', which is short for grasshopper. Oscar, who started that one, is lying on his back hugging his knees to his chest and seems to have a small crew copying him, including Parisa, who is Inisiya's little sister. Oscar looks like

a clunky Pied Piper, because he's making trumpet sounds
with his mouth to indicate position changes.

I leave Harold Barton talking to Inisiya and go over to
warn Caramella that he's turned up. I know she'll want to
try to persuade Mohammed to at least come and watch.
Then I make an announcement, introduce Harold and say
that anyone who's interested in doing juggling should cluster
around him after the warm-up.

It surprises me to see how many of them are interested.
All the boys, and also Inisiya, Nidal and, most unlikely of all,
Caramella. But Mohammed can't be coaxed out.

Harold Barton has brought along tennis balls as well as
juggling balls, so I figure we may as well all learn. But
Harold appears to be quite nervous at the prospect of taking
charge, and starts off in a stiff, awkward way, talking about
the principles of juggling.

I try to break the ice a bit by calling out, 'Give us a
demo!' so he does, and he's really very good. Even I'm
impressed. And you can tell by everyone's faces that their
eagerness levels just shoot upwards once they see what's
possible. That seems to energise Harold, who grabs a broom
and starts showing some stick-twirling. By the time he gets
us all standing against the wall, practising our throws, he's
relaxed, and everyone is calling to him to come and check
out their throws. They all want to move on to three balls.
But Hopper, of course, is jumping about and chucking balls
at people's bums.

What happens next happens so quietly that if I wasn't such a keen observer I might have missed it. First, Caramella approaches Harold Barton. I've never before seen those two even talk to each other, so of course I watch closely. She's talking quite intently, hands moving in the air. He has cocked his head to listen. After a while he nods and they part. She goes over to work with the Hmong girls and he attends to Sali. Then he grabs three balls, and walks over towards the door.

It's only then that I notice Mohammed standing there, wearing his little frown. Harold approaches him, talks, does a quick demonstration, then gives the balls to Mohammed and points towards a spot on the wall. Mohammed stands with the balls in his hands, staring down at them as if he's not sure how they got there, but since they are there, it seems, they lead him in. It makes me think of this story where there's a girl who puts on some red shoes and they make her dance. It's like that with Mohammed and those balls; they pull him in and then he's there. He gazes around wildly, as if he's afraid, but when he sees that no one has even noticed he seems to settle a bit, to let his weight sink into his feet, and then he begins throwing, carefully, quietly, also determinedly.

Caramella is watching surreptitiously and so is Harold, and even I can't help glancing over. Inisiya rushes up to me with eyes bulging.

'Look,' she whispers 'look at Mohammed.'

'I know.'

'It's amazing.'

We both stand there watching as Harold Barton gives some guidance to Mohammed, who tries with three balls, manages one round, and then drops a ball. As he picks it up, his eyes are suddenly ablaze and his whole face comes up smiling.

Smiling!

'You see that? He smiles!' cries Inisiya.

I look at Inisiya and then at Caramella and all three of us can't wipe the smiles off our own faces. In fact I feel like cheering, but I hold back. Harold Barton claps his hand on Mohammed's shoulders and nods as he walks away.

'It's the most unlikely thing in the world,' I say, kind of to myself, or to the world.

'What? That Mohammed would ever smile?' says Inisiya.

'No. Well, maybe. More that Harold Barton would be the one he smiled at.'

'Why?' says Inisiya, and then I remember that she doesn't know Harold, and because I don't want to ruin the good impression he's making I shake my head.

'Harold seems nice, though,' says Inisiya as she races over to tell Nidal what we just witnessed.

I stand there, watching. It's as if I've floated up into another stratosphere. Actually, I don't even know what a stratosphere is, but if there is another one I feel like I'm in it. It's as if I'm separate from what's going on, even though

I'm right in the middle of it. Mohammed's smile, although such a tiny, tiny crack, has opened up some unimaginably huge and invisible surface and I've floated up through it.

It feels as though I've just found a better trapeze than the one Frankie was hanging from, because it isn't mine, and it isn't anyone's. It's like a hammock of expanding and linking hearts that has joined together without knowing; from Aunt Squeezy to Inisiya to Caramella to Ruben and even to Harold Barton. All of them who've simply been willing to try to understand someone else.

I am so proud. I feel like a very small portion of the universe has shifted and no one is taking any applause. It is quite unspectacular and gloriously beautiful, and there I am, swinging from that moment like some kind of drunken gardener perched on an imaginary tree, feeling amazed by the splendour of the surrounding garden.

Meanwhile, no one even knew what had happened. Probably Mohammed would never know how much it meant to me to see him smile, or at least what it did to me after that.

Chapter 43

I skip in the door after training and Mum says, 'Kite called. He wants you to call him back. I wrote down the number.'

I stop dead still and I feel like laughing. For the first time all week I haven't been wishing he'd call. It's always the way.

I wait for Mum to leave the kitchen and then I call. I'm not even feeling nervous because somehow I'm in a mood where I feel a little bit less precious about my own life. Kite picks up the phone.

'Hey, Kite, it's me, Cedar.'

'Cedar.' He says my name like it's a slow sigh of a word.

'How are you?' I say.

'I'm fine. I'm sorry I haven't rung earlier. I wasn't sure if you wanted to talk to me or not.'

'Why wouldn't I?' (Note the bravado.)

He pauses and I picture him frowning.

'I thought you might have been upset about not getting selected. I wasn't sure…'

I make it easy for him. 'You mean you didn't want to deal with a weeping fit?'

'No, no, I mean yes, I would have – I just wasn't sure how, but it doesn't matter now because I've got some great news. They're offering you a place after all. The other girl couldn't take it up. Her father got a job in Melbourne. They're moving.'

'So they're offering me the place?'

'Yeah. Dad let me ring and tell you. How great is that? Can you take it?'

I know what I'm going to say, but before I say it I have some straight talking to do.

'Kite, if I took it, would I be, you know, cramping your style? With Lola I mean?' (Harder than I thought to talk straight.)

'Lola! Oh God, you know me better than that. You know I wouldn't be interested in a girl like Lola.'

There's another pause. Then a sigh.

'It's Frankie,' he says.

'Frankie?' I feel suddenly like I just lost the jousting spirit. My courage seems to fall away. Of course it was Frankie. Frankie was lovely, and besides, she could fly.

'Yeah, I guess Frankie and I had something going on when you came up. It was difficult because I didn't know… I didn't know what you wanted or thought…'

'No. Well, I didn't either. And I didn't know what you wanted.'

This time there's a silence; a long enough one for it to start to become loud and deep, like a black hole. Eventually I try to climb out of it. I sigh.

'So are you with Frankie now?'

'No.'

'Why not?'

'Oh, because I wasn't ever sure. Anyway, then you came up. Things got messy. Didn't seem like a good idea in the end; we have to see each other all day every day.'

I think I'm hurt, I'm not sure. I see myself pulling inwards and around me the quiet seems larger and larger. I don't know what to say so I don't speak. Instead, there's another crunching silence. This time it's Kite who sighs.

'Look, I'm sorry. Maybe we need to make things clear. I mean, between us.'

'I can't take the place. In the circus.' I burst out with it.

'Because of this? Because of Frankie?'

'No, because of Mohammed's smile.'

'What?'

'Oh, it's a long story. But basically I'm kind of committed to The Acrobrats now. I want to work with them. At least for this year. Then I'll see.'

'Are you sure? Maybe you should sleep on it.'

'No, I don't need to think about it, I'm sure.' (Oh God, am I temporarily insane?)

Kite says, 'Well, okay.'

And then there's another silence in which I can feel my

old dreams battling with my new feelings. I feel myself slipping into this battle. It's almost as if I forget I'm on the phone.

'Hey, Cedar – '

'Yeah?'

'I know you shouldn't do this on the phone, but I guess I want to clear this up. Do you want to go out with me? I mean, should we be together?'

I already know what I'm going to say to this too, but before I do I take a big breath and I close my eyes and I feel as if I'm on the very edge of something and I just want to stand at that edge and feel the great expanse of life before me.

'Yes.' My eyes have closed.

He laughs. Then I laugh.

He says, 'I wish I was there,' and I say, 'I wish you were too.'

And that's all I remember because after that I wasn't concentrating. I'd gone floating up again and I knew I wasn't mad.

Chapter 44

Of course, it wasn't just Mohammed's smile. It was Oscar's transforming blue rocks, it was Caramella's understanding heart, it was Aunt Squeezy's lessons on compassion, it was Inisiya's spirit and her story, the fact that everywhere there were stories you wouldn't have guessed. Grasshopper had one, Ada had one, even Harold Barton had one, and all this seemed to me to be where my living should be lived; in the messy, sad, huge, transforming muck that both bound us and separated us, not in the purely glorious heights of the circus.

Oh, don't worry, that circus dream still hovered there like a glass cloud above me, and one day I will climb up and grab it, but sometimes there's other stuff to be done before you're ready. It's like you have to build yourself a ladder; build the rungs out of real experiences. You have to know how to walk before you can fly. You have to especially know how to fall down, get dirty and then pick yourself up again. Along the way, you'll find out what you want and how to lose what you want. You have to learn know how to be a friend and stand underneath, and believe that against all odds you might one day do a handstand.

Above all, you should stay with your dog.

All this can only be done on the ground. I explained it to Kite in a letter and I think he understood because he wrote back:

Cedar, I'm not sure I really get you, but I know that's what I love about you. You've your own man, and you'll always live your own life.

At the station

So, here I am at the train station, for the second time this week. It's two days before Christmas. Yesterday we all came to see Aunt Squeezy off. It was very sad and everyone cried, even Barnaby, who never cries. Or maybe he didn't cry, but he looked like he could. Aunt Squeezy told me she was proud of me for staying. She said if she has a red-headed baby, and she hopes she does, that baby's second name will be Cedar. I said thank you for teaching me about lentils and hope, and bigotry and differences, and she laughed and winked and waved her hand, which tinkled in the air from the silver bracelets. Mum put her arm around me as we waved goodbye, and I think she was as sad as me to see Aunt Squeezy go.

Now I'm here again. It's warm. I'm wearing the green sundress that I mentioned earlier, but what I didn't tell you is how it has a white edge on the bottom and along the top, where it dips down in a very sexy way.

my train station outfit.

I also have some dark sunglasses on so I feel quite grown-up. It's making me walk in a certain way too, as if I'm sure. And, actually, I am. I am sure. It happens every now and then. It's like you and the day and your intentions meet up in perfect harmony and sing out a good loud note that's just right – not too loud or sharp, just right. And today, as I walk down the platform in my green sundress and my dark sunglasses, I feel sure it's a good-note day.

I know you can already guess who's arriving on the train just by the fact that I'm wearing something special. But I want to say it in a particular way. Like this:

It's my boyfriend.

My boyfriend.

Those two words together just keep putting more and more of a spring in my step. I kind of wish I might bump into someone, like say Marnie Aitken, or even just some old lady would do, though Marnie would be better, but still anyone. Someone who would ask, 'And what are you doing here?' and I'd say, 'Oh, I'm just meeting *my boyfriend*.' I'd say it in a casual way, though, just as if it was a normal thing to do, and they'd think, 'Oh, she's lucky, she's lucky to be meeting *her boyfriend*. And if that someone stood around to watch the train roll in they'd see the doors open and the guards come down with the luggage trolley, and the girl in the green dress take off her glasses and sit on a bench watching the passengers pour out, and there's a chunk of sun she's sitting in, which makes her red curly hair shine, and then she smiles because she has seen *her boyfriend*, but she doesn't stand up, not right away because he's already standing there in front of her with a bag slung over his shoulder and she wants to just look at him for a moment, since he's quite a handsome boy in a rough kind of a way, with nice brown arms that drop the bag just as she stands up, and then those nice brown arms wrap themselves around her and she leans up on her tiptoes and puts one arm over his shoulder and then they kiss. And at this stage the person watching turns away, because she feels it isn't the kind of kiss that you should watch for too long, so she walks off down the platform and goes to the newsagent where she buys herself a romance novel instead.

Acknowledgements

I would like to acknowledge the support of Anne Horrigan-Dixon and Sarah Maher at the Fitzroy Learning Network. Thank you for letting me come and see the great work you do and meet all the wonderful people who go there, especially Sara, who showed me how brave people can be.

Also I would like to acknowledge The Flying Fruit Fly Circus and Kim Walker who let me visit and watch, and made me wish I was still doing cartwheels.

A big thank you to Marnie Cruickshank, who lives on a cattle station in the west and wrote me the best letter in the world.

To Antoni Jach, thanks again for your support and encouragement, and to Sally Rippin, thanks for everything.

As usual, thank you Rosalind and Sue with whom it is a joy to work, and thank you to the dodgy hearts club with whom it is a joy to live.